The Girl

in the

Fall-Away

Dress

The Girl

in the

Fall-Away

Dress

STORIES

Michelle Richmond

University of Massachusetts Press   Amherst

This is a work of fiction, and any resemblance
to persons living or dead is coincidental.

This book is the winner of the Associated Writing Programs 2000 Award
in Short Fiction. AWP is a national, nonprofit organization dedicated
to serving American letters, writers, and programs of writing.
AWP's headquarters are at George Mason University, Fairfax, Virginia.

LC 2001002724
ISBN 1-55849-315-8

Designed by Kristina Kachele
Set in 10/15 Scala with FF Meta and Baker Script display.
Printed and bound by Sheridan Books, Inc.

Library of Congress Cataloging-in-Publication Data
Richmond, Michelle, 1970–
The girl in the fall-away dress : stories / Michelle Richmond.
p. cm.
"Winner of the Associated Writing Programs 2000 award in short fiction"
—T.p. verso.
ISBN 1-55849-315-8 (alk. paper)
1. United States—Social life and customs—20th century—Fiction.
I. Title.
PS3618.135 G57 2001
813'.6—dc21
2001002724
British Library Cataloguing in Publication data are available.

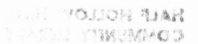

FOR KEVIN

Acknowledgments

Several of these stories originally appeared in the following
journals and anthologies:
"A Criminal History" in *Virgin Fiction* 2, edited by Eugene Stein
    (New York: William Morrow, 1999)
"Curvature" in *Brevity* 5 (1999)
"Down the Shore" in *Glimmer Train Stories* 41 (2001)
"The Girl in the Fall-Away Dress" in *Other Voices* 13, no. 33 (2000)
"The Last Bad Thing" in *Gulf Coast* 8, no. 2 (1996)
"Propaganda" in *The Florida Review* 23, no. 2 (1998)
"Satellite" in *CutBank* 52 (2000)

For giving me time and space to write, I want to thank King Yiu,
Dalian Moore, The Millay Colony, the Constance Saltonstall
Foundation, and the James Michener Foundation. My sincerest
appreciation also goes to the Associated Writing Programs and the
University of Massachusetts Press.

Thanks to Jiri Kajanë for his fine and infectious sense of the
absurd; to my sister Misty for her patient reading of my work over
the years; and above all to Kevin Phelan, a fine editor and great
storyteller, whose hair is an inspiration to us all.

Contents

The Girl

in the

Fall-Away

Dress

O-lama-lama

*a*ngel's mother makes red velvet cakes and talks about the prowess of God. In addition to this she speaks in tongues. Mrs. Brady has never in forty years cut her hair and it is a mountain on top of her head. She says to Angel, "Maybe your Baptist friend will convert."

Angel's father taps the phones in his house so he will know if his wife commits adultery, if his daughter talks to boys. Every morning before Angel leaves for school, Mr. Brady stands drowsily in the doorway of her bedroom and orders her to turn. She performs a lazy pirouette while he inspects her uniform. More often than not, he delivers a passionate lecture on the proper length of skirts before releasing her into the world.

At the little church by the beach in Fairhope, Angel and I sit in the back row. We keep our eyes open during prayer, not wanting to miss a thing. Halfway through the service Angel's father runs up to the pulpit and starts babbling. *O-lama-lama-ana-bacha-sabbatine-wyo*, he shouts. Mrs. Brady cries out and shakes her hips. Her hair falters but does not fall. *O-lama-lama*, Mr. Brady says, more quietly now, like a prayer. Tears run down his face. His shirt is drenched in sweat.

The preacher starts a conga line and within moments most of the church has joined in. The conga line weaves its way in and out of the pews, up to the baptistery, where everyone gets wet. The church is on a budget so the baptistery water is cold. Grown men emerge from the dyed blue water slick and shiny, their ties askew and dripping, their bare feet white and swollen. Ladies shiver and shout Amen, the seams of their Montgomery Ward bras showing through their satin blouses.

I follow Angel to the front of the church, where she takes two tambourines from a cardboard box that still bears its proud brand name: General Electric. Now, as before, the box contains the promise of good things to come—of love and enlightenment poured down like fresh water on this burning, beat-you-up life. We stand in front of the pulpit and dance like the freckle-faced girl on *The Partridge Family*. We shake our hips and snap our fingers and bang the tambourines, singing a Partridge Family tune.

Later, back at the house, Mrs. Brady feeds us red velvet cake and says, "I just hope you understand the meaning, girls. The whole point is to praise the Lord."

Down

the Shore

Everything's

All Right

*W*e're driving through the Lincoln Tunnel en route to Jersey when Ivan turns off the tape player and puts his hand on my thigh. I know what this means. It means he's gearing up to tell me the story. He'll be telling it in a way that suggests he has never told me this story before, that he has never told it to anyone, that it's coming straight to me from his heart, where he has saved it all these years. Each time the story is a little different; he adds or subtracts a few details, spruces up the dialogue, increases or decreases the temperature of that March day in northern California by a couple of degrees. Every time he tells the story, he has a new hook, an improved first line. This whole day has been planned in homage to that story, the story of the greatest moment of his life. We've rented a car and are on our way to Asbury Park.

It occurs to me that this is the day I'm going to break up with him; there is no more putting it off. After four years, it seems fitting that we should end our relationship in Asbury Park on the occasion of his second pilgrimage, and it seems somehow more civil than if I were to break the news to him anywhere else—over dessert at Edgar's, say, or in bed at our Eighty-fifth Street apartment.

Ivan first traveled to Asbury Park in 1982, soon after the release of *Nebraska*, three years after supposedly meeting Bruce Springsteen on a service road in San Mateo, California. He had gone to the Jersey Shore with his brother, driven cross-country from San Francisco hoping to get a glimpse of the world beyond the West Coast, and, more important, the world of Bruce. At the time, I was fourteen years old and a big fan of Madonna, and the crowd I ran with thought of Bruce as some overly patriotic guy with a redneck heart and a sweaty bandana. Bruce was a Jersey thing; being from the Gulf Coast, we didn't get it.

"There's this booth right on the boardwalk," Ivan says, fumbling with the hem of my skirt. "Madame Marie. I hope she's still there. Madame Marie read my palm, you know. She said I'd meet a girl with ringlets in her hair."

"Did you?"

"Not that I recall. But I did have this girlfriend named Sandy Cho who went to a Halloween party as Shirley Temple."

We exit the tunnel amid a cloud of exhaust fumes. An Atlantic City–bound bus screeches and sighs in front of us. This morning, Sam Champion on Channel Seven promised light showers in the city, heavy wind and rain on the Jersey Shore.

"I've gotta show you the Stone Pony. That's where Bruce met the band—Gary W. Tallent, Danny Federici, The Big Man, Vini Mad Dog Lopez, Miami Steve Van Zant. And we've got to see the Tunnel of Love, of course. Remember that song?" He sings it for me. *"Fat man sitting on a little stool, takes the money from my hand while his eyes take a walk all over you . . .* Did I ever tell you I got a picture of him?"

"You might have mentioned it."

"Too bad about the film."

When I first met Ivan, I thought the Bruce bit was a fish story he'd eventually let go of, a sort of introductory hoorah intended to impress me, like those guys who woo you with expensive restaurants only to settle into pizza-by-the-slice and Chinese-in-a-box as soon as they have your attention. I was a college girl from Alabama, visiting New York City for the first time. Ivan bought me dirty martinis at a place called Sabrina's, and we talked until the lights went down and a waitress in blue tights asked us to leave. Ivan also had stories about going to a Kings game with Tom Hanks and meeting Huey Lewis at a party, stories that came up only once, off-handedly, never to be repeated. But he has held tightly to his story about Bruce and the camera with no film, never budging, recounting it once or twice a year for various audiences, as if by sheer pig-headedness and repetition he might make it true.

He rolls down the window and the smell of New Jersey invades the car, industrial and sad and vaguely mean-spirited, a lingering fog of factory smoke and hair spray. Everything looks dismal from the passenger seat, where I am silently rehearsing my break-up speech.

"I'm exiting the drive-through at McDonald's," Ivan begins.

"I thought you said it was Taco Bell," I say, testing him, hoping to catch him in a lie.

"No, definitely McDonald's. I've got a Big Mac in my lap, a large Coke propped between my knees. There's this Mustang stopped in front of me. Another car has pulled in alongside him, and they're talking, blocking the intersection. I honk and the guy in the Mustang waves a hand out the window, like an apology, says goodbye to his friend, and pulls out. And I'm thinking, wow, I know that voice. That 'Bye, now,' I've heard it before. Bruce said it when he exited the stage at Winterland. But I'm a seventeen-year-old kid, right? And this guy's my idol, and I don't believe for a second it could be true."

"I once met Elizabeth Montgomery when I was waiting tables in

Tuscaloosa," I say, but Ivan's so caught up in the miracle of the remembered moment that he doesn't hear me, or at least my words don't register.

It doesn't take long for the turnpike to become less appalling. Smokestacks slowly disappear, giving way to heavily wooded road-sides and expansive medians, the first green I've seen in months. Pale, immaculate roofs peek over the tops of ugly sound barriers, and I think of the people in those regular houses, living regular lives, the kind I felt destined for until Ivan persuaded me to abandon wide southern beaches for big city sidewalks. Half of my motive for break-ing up with him is that I blame him for bringing me to New York City, where living quarters are minuscule and people are unkind. The other half is that I'm tired of his stories. Not just Bruce, but the others. Like the time he was walking down the street and saw a group of workmen handling a huge plate glass window several sto-ries above, and in the next instant the glass was suddenly airborne and falling, shattering inches behind him.

"A split second difference in my pace," he once told me, "a mo-ment of hesitation as I walked, and the window would have taken off my head." It seems to me the stuff of fantasy, his frequent meetings with celebrities and his hair-breadth escapes from death. Ivan lives in a dramatic world of his own making, in which he is a magnet for the incredible and the impossible, simultaneously inviting the mi-raculous and the macabre. The bottom line is this: I do not believe him. In the beginning his stories charmed me. Now, they only annoy me. I want him to be honest, dependable, perhaps a little mundane. I want to be the one person to whom he feels compelled to tell the truth. And there is the lingering fear that there are other, less inno-cent lies—lies relating to the weekend trips to Quebec with other teachers from his school, lies to explain the frequent and panicked voice of his ex-girlfriend on our answering machine.

"Once we're on the service road I pull up beside the Mustang, you know, just to check it out," Ivan continues. "There he is. It's Bruce.

I'm not believing it. He's got Gary U.S. Bonds singing 'Rendezvous' on the tape deck. So I roll down my window and yell, 'Bruce,' and he looks over at me and gives me this wave. Real stupid, I shout, 'Welcome to San Mateo!' and he starts motioning for me to pull over. I do, and he does, and he gets out of the car, and then he's shaking my hand. I've got this point-and-shoot in the glove compartment, and when I ask him if I can take a picture he says, 'Sure, why not.' If there had been film in the camera I'd have a picture of Bruce in a plaid flannel shirt and ripped jeans, just standing there looking slightly amused, with Togo's in the background. He's on his way to San Jose, but he says, 'Why don't you give me your phone number. I'll call you.' So I write it on the back of a crusty old road map, and then he pulls out, and I'm thinking, there's no way that just happened."

I finish the story for him, because I know the last line. No matter how it starts, it always ends the same way. "Greatest moment of your life," I say.

"Not any more. Second greatest moment of my life."

"What was the first?"

"Day I met you." He leans over and kisses me on the cheek, and I feel about this small, and I'm wondering how I'm going to pull off the break-up speech. And then I think maybe Asbury Park is all wrong, because it's a place he loves and if I break up with him there, maybe the place itself will be tainted. I should have thought of that before. I should have considered his theory of cross-contamination, how a thing can only be special in one kind of way. According to his theory, you don't take your new girlfriend to the same vacation spot you went with the old girlfriend, and you never fall in love with a woman who has the same first name as someone you loved before. It stands to reason, then, that he doesn't believe in making bad memories in a place where you've already made good ones.

"I have something to tell you," I say.

He cranks up the radio. "Out with it, bubba." That's what he calls me sometimes, bubba, because I'm from Alabama.

7

"I can't do this anymore."

"Do what?"

"This. Us."

He looks over at me, laughing. "Very funny. No, really. What did you want to tell me?"

"I'm serious."

He looks at me again. There's a tiny mole on the curve of his chin I never noticed before, not in four years of looking at him up close. "You're kidding me."

"It's just not working."

We pass a hitchhiker in green corduroy pants. Her sign says she'll pay half the gas. "I spy me a hitchhiker," I say, trying to lighten the mood with a game Ivan and I used to play on our frequent road trips. "I spy me a rabbit." The rule is that you can spy anything as long as it's animate, and the first one to repeat something loses.

"What do you want me to do?" Ivan says. "You want to move? You want to get married? We'll get married if that's it. We'll move out of the city. Get a place in Asbury Park, maybe, you'll like it there, it's real quiet in the winters. Or go down South. You want to go down South?"

"That won't solve it."

"Where's this coming from? What did I do?"

"You didn't do anything."

Silence, except for Howard Stern on the radio. He's interviewing a leading child psychologist, quizzing her on the size of her breasts. He wants to know if her breasts get in the way of her social work. She wants to know if his stupidity gets in the way of his career. She postulates that Howard Stern was breast-fed until the age of ten or so and thus his fascination with the mammary gland. She suggests that he wants to sleep with his mother. "Whoa-ho!" Howard says. "Easy, baby. I'll tell you who I want to sleep with. I want to sleep with *your* mother!" Howard's sidekick, Robin, tells him to behave.

"Maybe we should turn around," I say.

"We've come this far. We've got the car for the day. May as well."

A couple of minutes later we exit the turnpike, then drive in silence for a long time toward the shore. It begins to rain. The windshield wipers of our plastic rent-a-car keep sticking, and every couple of minutes I have to lean out the window and lift the wipers from the glass to get them moving again.

Our route takes us through broken-down towns that all look pretty much the same: old factories with soot-scarred windows, bent cars parked permanently in driveways, filthy little grocery stores with big white banners in the windows advertising pork roast and Pampers. Ivan watches the slick road while I watch the odometer. It clicks off the miles with a slowness that reminds me of Alabama, Sunday drives with my parents and sisters through green empty places that inevitably ended at some abandoned length of railroad, the crossing signals long defunct. At one point Ivan reaches over and opens the glove compartment, then fumbles for a cassette. When he does this I move my knees aside, but the rental car is small and it's impossible not to touch. His hand brushing the back of my knee feels natural for about half a second, and then it's just embarrassing. He jerks it away, like I'm made of fiberglass or fire, and says, "See if you can find *Darkness On the Edge of Town*."

As the opening song plays, Ivan's hands beat the steering wheel, only vaguely in rhythm with the music. It's been about twenty miles since he looked my way. I know the story that goes with this song, how this was the first album he ever bought. How he took it home and put it on the turntable in the bedroom he shared with his brother at his family's new house in Burlingame, then listened to it for an entire day, the same song, hundreds of times.

Halfway through the song he pops the cassette out of the player. "How about the Stockholm tape?" he says. I fish through the glove compartment and find it. Bruce's version of "Jersey Girl," by Tom Waits, is playing as we pull into Asbury Park. *Now baby won't you come with me, cause down the shore everything's alright, you and your baby on a Saturday night. Nothing matters in this whole wide world when you're in love with a Jersey girl. Sing sha la la la la . . .* Like most of Bruce's own songs, "Jersey Girl" is two parts hope, one part working-man blues, and another part lusty despair.

A red Camaro passes on our left. The driver, a middle-aged woman with tattoos down the length of her arm, gives us a happy wave, then guns the engine and moves on ahead. After Bruce, we hear Tom Waits doing the same song in his low-down rumble. When Tom Waits sings "Jersey Girl," you get the feeling that nothing is all right anywhere, and nowhere is less all right than where you are right now.

The rain is coming down hard, and the wind is pushing our two-door all over the road. The whole town looks deserted. You can tell from the crumbling facades of big, handsomely built hotels that wealthy people once vacationed here, then abandoned the place when it ceased to be fashionable. We park at a shut-down gas station across the street from the Tunnel of Love. The tunnel is nothing more than a hole carved into a low cement wall, the entrance deco-rated with a fading mural. I remember my second kiss ever—in the haunted house ride at Six Flags over Georgia. The guy's name was Jason Lowery. He put his hand up my shirt as our vehicle tipped toward a vast hall of floating skeletons. I felt a strange electricity on my skin, hundreds of tiny pinpricks circling my nipple.

"There used to be a drive-in theater back there," Ivan says, point-ing somewhere beyond the decrepit amusement ride. "Did I ever tell you about the freeway drive-in?"

I shake my head no rather than answering aloud, just to force him to look at me. He doesn't.

"When I was in grammar school, my parents had this house above Daly City. From the window of our bedroom my brother and I could see the screen of the Geneva Drive-In across the freeway. Late at night, when we were supposed to be asleep, we'd lean out the window and watch the show. They played mostly sex flicks. We couldn't hear any sound, so we'd make up our own words. Blonde girls with enormous tanned breasts and plump red mouths saying things like, 'I think it's the carburetor' or 'Beam me up, Scotty.' "

I imagine him, age seven, with that bushy black hair I've seen in his old school photos. He's leaning out the window, his small face intersected by the shadows of a gigantic film, his features transformed frame by frame as naked bodies shift on the screen.

Rain is leaking through the passenger side window onto my lap. Ivan takes off his windbreaker and arranges it over my legs. "You ever go to the drive-in?"

"We didn't have one in Mobile. If you wanted to see a movie, you had to go to Springdale Mall."

We talk about movies for a while, and then about what they call the New South, how it's short on character and big on strip malls. I recount for him the steeple wars waged by the Southern Baptist churches of my childhood, how my parents emptied their pockets each week to contribute to the war chest of Bay Street Baptist Church, how the new steeple towered over Mobile Bay, white and gleaming like a sword.

Then we talk about a weekend we once spent in Monte Rio, when Ivan got sick from Swedish pancakes at the River Inn. "Remember swimming out to the little island?" Ivan asks. For a moment we are both lost in the sweet-smelling warmth of the river, the memory of it running narrow and swift behind the inn. That night we hauled cold beer to the sandbar in a small Styrofoam chest, then lay on our backs and watched cars pass on the highway that hugged the high banks of the river. It's strange how a relationship can go on living for hours after you both know it's dead, how we can sit here and talk about nothing as if everything's the same, as if there are no decisions to be made.

When the rain lets up, Ivan starts the car and we drive about a mile down the shore. We park in front of a boarded-up building, nothing more than a wooden box really, with a roof made of corrugated tin.

"Madam Marie, World Famous Psychic" is painted in big red letters on the side of the shack. We walk past Madam Marie's onto the boardwalk. I'm wearing Ivan's windbreaker with the hood pulled tight around my face. My short summer skirt whips up around my thighs. Ivan's wearing only a button-down and jeans, but the cold doesn't seem to bother him. He likes wet weather; the harder the rain, the better. It's the ambiguous days that depress him: when the sun is out but it's windy anyway, and the temperature wavers indecisively between hot and cold. San Francisco days, he calls them.

The rain has slowed to a drizzle, but the wind is roaring off the gray Atlantic so hard the boardwalk shifts beneath us. "Beautiful," Ivan says, leaning on the wooden rail to stare out at the ocean. "Could you live here?"

"Maybe," I say, but I'm thinking it's colder here on an April afternoon than any winter day I remember in the city. I've never seen a beach so austere, just a narrow strip of sand retreating from an angry ocean. On the Gulf Coast the water spans out blue and bright for miles, but here the fog hangs low and the world doesn't seem to stretch much farther than my fingertips. I don't know if it's mere habit or a slim attempt at apology that makes me reach for Ivan's hand. He accepts, and we wander along the boardwalk in the rain and fog. It's only a quarter past two, but the sky is dark. I look over my shoulder every now and then, half expecting to see Madam Marie plodding along behind us, hands outstretched, her gold earrings flapping in the wind.

"He called me once," Ivan says

I'm thinking about packing, wondering if Gristede's at Eighty-fifth and Columbus puts its used boxes out by the curb. I'm trying to calculate how many boxes I'll need to move out. I estimate my life will fit neatly into four or five of the hefty ones from the grocer, still smelling of apples and alfalfa from upstate New York. That, plus a dozen or so smaller boxes from Pricewise at Amsterdam and Eighty-first, where the sturdy security man in his creased pants and lopsided nametag always greets me with a lifted eyebrow and a shout of "Hey Red."

"Of course I thought he'd never call," Ivan says. "I didn't hear from him for a couple of weeks. But then one night around midnight, I'm at home in bed. The phone rings and I reach for it, and a voice says, 'Is Ivan there?' "

I'm so caught up in the logistics of our break-up—when I'll leave, where I'll stay, whether or not I'll return home, the failed daughter lugging boxes and books over her parents' doorstep—that I don't realize where this story is headed.

" 'It's me,' I say. I'm half asleep and I assume, at this point, that I'm dreaming, because it can't be who I think it is.

" 'It's Bruce,' the voice says. 'Sorry to call so late.' He keeps apologizing. He's worried that he woke everybody up, like he's going to get me in trouble or something. 'Look,' he says, 'me and my sister were just driving around. We were gonna get something to eat. Want us to come pick you up?' "

"You never told me this before," I say.

"Would you have believed me?"

"No."

"That's why I didn't tell you."

"Why now?"

"Because now it doesn't matter."

I wonder how long he's been holding on to this story, if it's something he made up a long time ago, or if he's creating it at this moment, one last desperate fiction to win me back.

"In the dark I grope for a T-shirt and jeans, pull on my Pumas, then navigate the carpeted stairs and creep out the front door. It's March in the Bay Area, midnight, which means it's kick-ass cold, and I'm standing out by the curb in the dark, shivering in my T-shirt."

Ivan is leaning against the rail looking out at the sea, raindrops running down his face. His hair is soaked, but he doesn't seem to notice. The top half of my body is dry beneath the windbreaker, but my legs are wet and frozen. I place a hand on his arm and try to pull him away from the rail, toward the car; he doesn't move.

"I wait for what seems like a long time, although it was probably no more than fifteen minutes. I see a pair of headlights down Balboa Avenue, but the car turns onto Carmelita. I'm feeling really alone now, more alone than I've ever felt in my life, wondering what I'm doing on the curb outside my parents' house at midnight, waiting for the world's greatest living rock 'n' roll star to show up at my door. I tell myself it's a dream. As I'm turning to go inside I hear the low hum of a car engine a couple of blocks away. Then the headlights, and this time they turn down my street. The Mustang pulls up in front of my house. Bruce has the top down. His sister's in the passenger seat."

Ivan breaks away from the rail, turns, and jogs down the boardwalk toward our car. I follow. He unlocks my side first, then walks in no hurry at all over to his own. I'm shimmying into a pair of his sweatpants that I found in the backseat when he says, "There *is* a picture of us, you know. I wish I had it. I wish I could prove it to you."

"I thought you said there was no film in the camera."

"No, another picture. That night, we drove to Ken's House of Pancakes. We each got a quarter-pound burger with fries and coleslaw. I had a chocolate milkshake. While we were eating, Bruce's sister pulled a camera out of her purse. She was sitting beside Bruce, and she said to him, 'Go over there and sit next to Ivan.' He slid out of the booth and came over to my side and put his arm around my shoulders, like we'd been buddies for a long time."

He cranks the engine and a blast of cold air comes through the vents.

"Why are you doing this?" I say. "Why can't you just tell the truth?"

"I did tell my family the next morning. They didn't believe me. I've never told anyone since. I feel like those people from Roswell who claim to have been abducted. I don't blame you for not believing me, but at some point you just have to tell the story, no matter what people think."

Four days later, he helps me load my rented car. It's hard to know what belongs to whom, so I just take what I think I'll need: clothes, mostly, and books, my computer and VCR. The sleigh bed we bought at an antique store in Chelsea stays with him, as do three framed prints from the Stenberg Brothers exhibition at MoMA. We hug and kiss goodbye. There's no animosity and, contrary to what I had expected, no feeling of relief. Just a big emptiness, the way I used to feel when I had to turn in my roller skates at Dreamland Skating Rink after a birthday party, knowing it would be a long time before I returned, already missing the feel of the floor spinning beneath me, the thud of the disco music on the loudspeakers. Leaving Ivan, I try not to think about all the ways I'm going to miss him.

"What if I track her down?" he says, adjusting my sun visor. "What if I find Bruce's sister and by some miracle she still has the photo? Then you'd have to believe me."

"This is pathetic," I say, buckling my seat belt. "It's not normal. What's wrong with the life you have? Why do you have to make things up?"

I have two thousand miles to convince myself that dishonesty is a suitable reason to end a relationship, forty-plus hours to rationalize my obsession with the truth. I think about all those trips he made to Quebec without me, and the ex's voice on the machine. "*Call* me," she'd whine, each time he returned from one of those trips, as if she had a right to demand this, as if she had some hold on him. What I wanted most from him, I guess, was satisfaction. I wanted him to think that what we had together was a sufficient story.

Driving over the causeway into Mobile, I roll up the windows and close the vents against the gritty smoke of the paper mill, that wet and sour smell. In high school we used to escape the odor by burying our noses in plastic cups of rum and Coke as we sped over the causeway, headed toward the rowdy oyster bars and swank marinas across the bay. I wonder what happened to all those tall, sure boys whose fathers owned the boats I escaped to on Saturday nights, boys who knew exactly how to position a girl on the long vinyl couch below deck. The marina back then seemed a sacred place, out of reach of Bay Street Baptist Church and the Sunday school teachers who insisted that my body belonged first to God and second to my future husband. With the boats knocking against each other in the dark, my hands guiding other hands beneath the waistband of my jeans, I could almost believe my body belonged to me.

The heat is so intense by early April that it's difficult to breathe. Still, the steamy humidity feels right in a way New York's dry cold never did. I marvel at the calmness of the bay, the enormity of the World War II battleship that has hunkered there in the shallows for as long as I can remember. The traffic on the causeway eases along, old Cadillacs and Fords rumbling by with the windows down. I'm already beginning to feel at home again in this region of big American cars and pickup trucks, bait shops and motorboats. Tomorrow I'll drive down to the Gulf of Mexico, lay out a towel in the shadows of the sand dunes on the wide public beach. It will be nearly empty, nothing like Coney Island, and the water will be warm and tame enough for swimming, nothing like the Jersey Shore. I'll lie perfectly still and watch the sand crabs burrow into their ramshackle holes, listen to their frenzied activity beneath the surface of the sand. Then I'll walk down the beach and count the disfigured jellyfish washed up on shore, their plump transparent bodies tangled in Sargasso weed.

As the causeway grows longer behind me and Fort Conde looms ahead, the black cannons of the Revolution shining like playthings, I rehearse the speech I have prepared for my parents. I am certain they will be glad to see me, relieved that I have left "that awful city," which is the only name my mother has for New York.

DOWN THE SHORE EVERYTHING'S ALL RIGHT

At 4:00 in the afternoon I show up on their doorstep, haggard and half-asleep. I have to ring the doorbell like a stranger, because I no longer have keys to the house where I grew up. My mother answers the door. She's so happy she's laughing, until she notices my rental car in the driveway, packed so full the trunk is partially open, tied down with a length of rope.

"We liked him," she says over dinner. "David, didn't we like him?"

"You've been together, what, a couple of years?" my father says.

"Four," my mother corrects him.

My three sisters are grown and absent, pursuing lives in Texas, Tennessee, and Georgia. "Outward mobility" is the term my father uses to describe his daughters' slow but steady migration, one after the other until his five-bedroom house in Alabama's southernmost city came to resemble a storage locker more than a home. Each daughter's room, emptied of beds and essential clothing, contains plastic crates we keep meaning to go through, patterns for dresses we never made, shoes we can't bear to let go of, books we think we might learn from someday if we ever get the time: Darlene's American history textbooks from high school, Celia's French readers from college, Baby's *National Geographic* collection, my Modern Library series. Each of us left more behind than we took with us when we moved. There is a feeling of absence about the place, a lack of sound and movement all of our messy possessions can't make up for. Alone with my parents for the first time I can remember, I feel the house the way they must feel it: large and empty. With just the three of us here, the table seems massive.

"Maybe you can patch it up," my mother says, passing the peas over the wide expanse of glass. The table is supported by what looks like a giant conch shell, a monstrosity of plaster and flesh-toned paint. *Mobile Bay Monthly* has a name for this kind of table: Gulf Coast Chic. "Maybe you should apologize. Maybe he really did meet what's-his-name."

"Bruce."

"It's possible. Bruce puts on his pants, you know, just like the rest of us."

"What's that got to do with anything?"

"You're almost thirty, I'm just saying."

Within a few weeks I have a job and a steady date, someone I knew in high school who now works for his father's financial firm. In a couple of months the regression is complete: I've purchased a tiny, refurbished shotgun house on Church Street, half a block from the Mardi Gras parade route. It's cute and it cost next-to-nothing. My neighbors have frequent crawfish boils, to which I'm always invited. Some nights, they play Jimmy Buffet so loud his drunken lyrics must carry all the way across the bay to Fairhope. A tall, sandy-looking boy from Murphy High School mows my lawn in bare feet and cut-off Duckheads, taking beer breaks on my porch. He looks and talks and moves like every boy I dated in high school, a Southern gentleman in the making, patronizing and smooth. When I invite him inside, he sits right next to me on the couch, so close I can feel the sweat of his thigh through my thin cotton dress. He invites me to spend a weekend at his parents' house on Ono Island. I am shocked to find myself flirting, tempted by the offer.

Nine months after the break-up a UPS truck parks in front of my house. The box is from Ivan. To the inside of the box he has taped a note. *Dear Gracie, I'm moving back to San Francisco. Found some of your things when I was cleaning out the apartment. Hope all is well with you. Love, Ivan.*

The box contains sundry items of no consequence: floppy disks with outdated software, playbills from a few off-off Broadway shows, a water glass from John's Pizza, a file folder labeled Travel Ideas, stuffed with glossy magazine photos of Iceland and Peru. There is a manila envelope full of photographs that inspire a nostalgia I'm not prepared for. By the time I've finished looking at the photos—candid shots taken at subway stops, inside our cramped apartment, and at

B&Bs in the Poconos and northern Vermont—I'm trying to convince myself that I don't miss him like crazy, that leaving him wasn't the last and worst in a long line of bad decisions.

The final photo is one I've never seen before, a grainy 5×7 in black and white, portraying a much younger Ivan with longer hair. He looks tired, as if he's just woken from an insufficient sleep, but at the same time he looks alive, more alive than I've ever seen him. The photo is taken inside a restaurant and has been shot from across a table. There is writing on Ivan's T-shirt, but I can't read it, because a bottle of ketchup intersects the small words. He's sitting next to a guy, someone whose face I know from other photos, from television and magazines. It's a wiry Bruce with a three-day beard. He's wearing a faded sweatshirt with the sleeves rolled up, and he's smiling half a smile, maybe a little tired, but happy. Their booth is in front of a window, and in the background I can see the darkness of the parking lot, and beyond the darkness the green glow of a neon sign announcing Ken's House of Pancakes. I search the photo for seams, for signs that it's been doctored, inexplicable alterations in light and shadow. I study the hand draped over Ivan's shoulder, its proportions and probabilities. I search for a hairline of space separating their two bodies, and, finding none, I marvel at the intricacy of the lie, the precision of the ruse, the bold lengths to which Ivan has gone to keep his story intact.

Big

Bang

*M*yla Tarver's parents do not go to church. Sunday mornings you can see them working in their garden, hands and forearms sheathed in rubber gloves. By the time we pass in our Galaxy 500 en route to Bay Street Baptist Church, their knees are smudged with topsoil, their shoulders slightly burned. The front door of the house is open. Jim Croce and Joan Baez blast into the yard. Myla has confessed that her parents went to Woodstock, that they drove all the way from Arkansas to New York in a Volkswagen bus with no windshield. In the master bathroom there is a photo of Mrs. Tarver with no shirt, a man who isn't Myla's father smearing mud onto her breasts.

My sisters and I are crammed into the backseat in order of age. First Darlene, then Celia, me, and Baby. By the time we leave for church each week, our family is on the verge of collapse. Sunday morning preparations—showers and blow dryers and battles over who gets to go into Krispy Kreme to buy the doughnuts for continental breakfast—leave us angry and unkempt. Only my father emerges unscathed from the family fray, looking neat and polished in his navy suit, having spent the morning with his *Mobile Press Register*.

I lean over my sisters to roll the window down, hoping to catch a glimpse of Mrs. Tarver's famous breasts, and of Myla, whom I envy greatly, in her Sunday morning bliss. "Don't look, Gracie." My mother laughs uneasily. She seems to fear that I will become vicariously unchurched.

My father, hands on the wheel, is eyeing Mrs. Tarver, who raises a trowel and waves. Her tank top is cut off at the waist so you can see her belly button. "Nice azaleas," my father says, coming to a complete stop in front of their house.

Myla emerges through the front door. She has a glass of iced tea in one hand, a paperback book in the other, and is wearing a pair of sunglasses too big for her skinny face. "Hey Gracie, call me later," she shouts, plopping down in the front porch hammock.

"I don't want you calling her," my mother says, smiling at the Tarvers.

For a moment I imagine myself in Myla's place, sisterless and free. An only child, she holds the status in her family of a small and slightly irresponsible adult. Her parents find her witty. They indulge her voracious desire for jelly shoes in pastel colors, her occasional moral infractions. She is only eleven, a couple of months my senior, but she has already kissed three boys.

Mr. Tarver is trimming his gardenia bush. He lets the shears hang by his side and walks over to the car. "Hey girls," he says, peeking in.

"Hey," we say in unison, and the car is moving once again. We always seem to be snaking slowly forward, with no control over our direction.

"Why aren't they going to church?" Baby asks. Baby is four. The white lace that edges her nylon socks bears a bright pink Kool-Aid stain.

"Because they're lucky," Darlene says.

"They're misguided," my mother corrects her. "Darlene, where are your pantyhose? And didn't I tell you to shave?"

Darlene is fifteen. Her muscular calves stick out beneath the hem of her yellow seersucker dress. The dress looks all wrong. Darlene looks all wrong. "This sucks," she says.

My mother whips around in her seat and stops just short of slapping Darlene across the face. "Watch your language Miss Hateful. We're on our way to church."

Darlene glowers at her, triumphant. "That was almost child abuse."

My father, momentarily roused, glances at us in the rearview mirror, pats my mother on the knee, and says, "Let's everybody calm down."

I think of Myla in her hammock, sipping iced tea through a curly pink straw. While I'm in Sunday school discussing First Thessalonians, she'll probably be reading raunchy books by Judy Blume or talking on the phone long-distance. She's only here for a year while her father is on sabbatical from the University of Arkansas, where he is a professor of history. My mother says it's a sad thing to have your head in the past with the Rapture rapidly approaching. Myla is the first friend I've ever had whose parents don't believe in God.

When I spend the night with Myla we stay up late in her big wicker bed, and Myla tells me dangerous stories of how the world came to be. In Myla's stories there is no Adam and no Eve, no silver-tongued snake vying for Eve's affection. I like lying under the cool sheets with Myla, our knees softly touching, the door shut on our own private world.

Myla hopes to be a great scientist. She talks of research and great big laboratories, microscopes that can reveal the intimate mysteries of a cell. My mother says that's nice, but for us she has higher aspirations: she wants us to become missionaries and roam the ends of the earth. She wants us to do all the traveling she never did.

"Scientists are confused," she says. "They spend their lives trying to explain things we already know, trying to find answers we already have." By "we" she means those who can hear clearly the voice of God.

Satellite

*S*ven is on the roof. I can hear him stomping around up there, doing what he does best. He has come with his satellite dish, his big red box of tools, his six years of experience, his generous heart. He is installing a dish for my father, the historian. "Hey Myla, I got a great deal on this thing," Sven said last night, proudly unboxing the dish for me back at his house on Garland, a half-mile down the road from the university where my father teaches. "Think he'll like it?"

"He doesn't have a television."

"No sweat. I've got a bunch. He can have the nineteen-inch. It's three years old but it works fine." For Sven, television years run alongside dog years. At nine months a set is mature, by four years it's on the downswing, once it hits six you simply keep it around out of compassion, loyalty, familial respect. Sven could fashion the innards of a television out of coat hangers and string if necessary, but he could not work an oven to stave off starvation.

My father cannot help but be uneasy with a man who is so resolute in his bachelorhood, holding on to the old ways. Even before my mother died, my father could whip up a remarkable roulade or baste a turkey to perfection. His clothes are much better-ironed than my own, his china cabinet more attractively stocked. I am convinced the reason I survived my mother's demise so well was that the household continued to run efficiently in her absence. I was twelve years old when lightning struck her in Little Rock, one of those freak accidents you hear about and hardly believe, "Three hundred people killed by lightning in the United States each year." According to the newspaper article, my mother was number two hundred thirty-nine. When I first told Sven how she died he thought it was a joke. A piano teacher from Fayetteville, Arkansas—mother of one, painter of landscapes, collector of paperweights—just doesn't die like that. The lightning bolt struck the tree under which she and her best friend Judy had taken shelter from a rainstorm on the third day of their sixteenth annual visit to the capital. They were sitting on a bench. Judy was unharmed and my mother died. According to Judy, my mother had refused to sit on the side of the bench closest to the metal garbage can, opting instead to sit directly beneath the tree's lowest-hanging limb.

After she died I waited for everything to fall apart, but it didn't. Although I never stopped missing her, eventually I came to realize that it had always been my father who kept the house and family intact. I returned to school three days after her funeral, my hair properly combed, the whiteness of my socks and uniform shirt uncompromised.

One winter when the pipes burst and flooded the basement I came home from a weekend in the Ozarks with my high school boyfriend Jason—one in a long string of promising athletes—to find my thin, graceful father ankle deep in the frigid water, mopping, while a hired man repaired the pipes. I know he must look at Sven and see a hopeless case, some anthropological holdover from the days when men took out the trash and women explored the endless possibilities of casseroles.

Sven moved to Fayetteville two years ago with no furniture and no friends, only a vague history with lots of blanks he's not eager to fill in. I was born here and never came up with any good reason to move away; there is something comforting about the place, with its low hills and seasonal weather, its constant influx of university kids from rural Arkansas. I see Dad at least once a week and Sven often accompanies me, content to participate in the routines that have become my life. He is not trying to win my father over with the satellite dish; bribery would never occur to him, just as it would not occur to him that my father might not like him. Dislike, anyway, would be much too strong a word. My father doesn't understand Sven, but he is in no way averse to him.

My father has spent the last fifteen years of his life compiling the letters of Wendell Cage, a labor of love that has netted him several thousand dollars in grant money, four sabbaticals from the history department where he is a tenured professor, and an unpublished five-volume set of correspondence that threatens to become seven volumes before the project is finished. Wendell Cage was as prolific with his letters as he was with his children: twenty-eight by two wives and four mistresses, a clean number until you break it down on a per-mom basis. The mistresses produced twenty-two of the kids, far more than their fair share. Little remains of the man save an old plantation house in Eufala, Alabama, two unremarkable works of entomology, one uncelebrated novel titled *In A Cold Place*, and the letters.

My father came upon the novel at The Haunted Bookshop in Mobile a few months after my mother's death. He purchased it because he liked the binding, immediately recognizing it as the work of a long-defunct confederate publishing house whose trademark was a cotton plant stamped a half-inch from the bottom of the spine. My father bought the novel as a relic only, an homage to the past; but once he had read it he immediately devoted himself to Cage, convinced beyond doubt that this man whose name he had never heard was the greatest American writer of the nineteenth century.

SVEN AND I have only been going out for three months, but at some point we fell into a routine whereby I spend most nights at his place. Mornings Sven gets up around six o'clock and showers, and I pretend to sleep while he dresses silently by the window, trying not to wake me. It is a pleasure to see him unwrapping the towel from his trim waist, and then to watch the muscles of his buttocks shift when he bends to take his underwear off the chair. After putting on his jeans he always turns toward the full-length mirror beside the bed, raising his arms above his head to put on a clean white T-shirt. During those moments when he is unknowingly exposed I concentrate on the cleft in the center of his chest just below the sternum, a deep indentation the circumference of a quarter.

This morning I went back to sleep after watching him dress, then got up an hour later and made coffee, brewing it dark the way he likes. I found Sven outside, loading the big cardboard box containing the satellite dish into the back of his pick-up truck. The television was there as well, swaddled in bubble wrap. I kicked at an oversized mushroom that had broken through the soft surface of the asphalt, exposing its hairy underside. "Let's call first and see if Dad wants it."

"Wants it?" Sven shouted joyfully. "Of course he wants it! Besides, I've already got it in the truck." Sven's success as a satellite dish salesman must have something to do with his ability to convince anyone of anything, despite the condition of all facts and favorable odds being against him; I am certain that people go along with him in part, like I do, because he gets so excited about something you can't imagine disappointing him.

Dad was at the mailbox when we pulled into the driveway, his hand thrust deep inside. When he withdrew his hand there was nothing in it, and I knew he would be disappointed today, distracted. He was waiting for a particular letter, the existence of which he had only recently discovered, a one-page item sent by Wendell Cage more than a century ago to a young woman in Germany named Helga von Trask. My father already translated the precursor to that document, a letter from the sixteen-year-old Helga to the sixty-three-year old Cage in which she informs him of her pregnancy. In her letter, Helga begs Cage to send her the money to join him in America.

Sven parked at the top of the driveway, got out, and shoved the box toward the tailgate. "Nice to see you, Sven," my dad said, reaching out to shake hands. But Sven was already busy slicing through the masking tape with his Swiss army knife. He ripped the box open and stood over his gift, beaming like a proud father. "With this sweet piece of machinery you'll be able to receive upwards of 200 channels."

Dad just stood there, looking surprised and amused, staring at the dish in its bed of packing worms. He turned to me and asked quietly, "I don't have a television, do I?" as if there might be one stuck away in some corner of the house he'd forgotten.

"Sven brought you one of those, too."

"Sorry, it's only a nineteen-inch, but the picture quality is good. RCA. Top of the line in its class three years ago. The dish, though, this baby's the sweet 'n' saucy end of the deal. Take a look. What you've got here is a 5451, built-in antenna. Bigger is definitely better. The bigger the dish, the more amplification."

"Amplification?" I asked, prodding Sven, wanting him to show off a little, wanting Dad to understand that despite his pickup truck and less than glamorous job, Sven has a head on his shoulders.

"Sure," he said, launching into a long monologue about the LNBF, how it catches the signal that bounces off the dish, amplifies it and converts the frequency, stuff I'd heard a few times before but that I never really get bored with, because I love to see a man in his element, employing the terms he knows best. When I was in junior high, I used to sit in a corner of my dad's office while he consulted with his students, watching him transform into a person entirely different from the one he was with me. I loved the way his female students stared at him, a little awed, while he went on about history or some work of literature he felt passionately about, seemingly unaware that his preacher-man voice and dark blue eyes had them under a spell. With his male students he struck a more casual tone, and he was slightly more intimate with the seniors than with the freshmen. He was another man altogether with his colleagues, and different with the professors in his own department than with those in the other humanities. Eventually I came to understand that his changing personality is not due to any duplicity or pretense on his part; he naturally slips into the personality that he believes will put a person most at ease.

When Sven is around, Dad tries to talk about sports or home repair, careful not to engage me in a conversation that Sven is unable to join. Sven, on the other hand, remains the same across the board, unchanging, one Sven for every occasion, solid as history. I could tell from the way Dad rocked back and forth on his heels that he was zoning out, unable to process Sven's explanation of azimuth and elevation angles, transponders and signal strength. He smiled politely and nodded his head, and Sven, believing that he and my father belonged to a worldwide fraternity of men fascinated by the intricate workings of television, took this as a sign of encouragement.

"The signal comes from 22,300 miles away at over twelve gigahertz. 22,300 miles! That's some space-age shit." He had set the dish down on the driveway and was caressing the antenna tenderly, the way Jason in eleventh grade used to caress his kayak, the way Devon my sophomore year of college handled the greasy matrix of machinery beneath the hood of a British sports car, the way Jimmy my senior year touched the game ball that bought him a ticket to the minors. Before Sven it had been Dave, and before Dave it was Greg. My romantic history is replete with men whose hands have moved as smoothly over my thighs and belly, my breasts and back, as they did over some cherished item that loudly proclaimed their manhood. It's embarrassing, really, the guys I go for. While my friends hook up with artists and intellectuals, men who know how to serve a flambé or choose a bottle of wine to go with the swordfish, men who kind of like the thought of being transformed at some point in their late thirties into stay-at-home dads, I am a sucker always for the well-cut abs, the strong jaw, the height and heft and sturdiness of any nice guy six feet and over with traditional male sensibilities.

In high school my father assumed it was a distasteful phase I would simply grow out of. Not until I was halfway through college did he begin trying to hook me up with his graduate students, studious boys he'd introduce me to at department parties, boys who overflowed with knowledge about some specific point in history that invariably had to do with war or uprising: Hunt and the Civil War, Jack and the French Revolution, Sid and Nazi Germany, George and the Bolsheviks. These guys had monosyllabic names and scholarly if not somber demeanors. They nibbled sesame sticks laced with vegetable dip and drank wine out of plastic cups, utterly at home in the rather understated elegance of Arkansas academia. They asked me all about my interests rather than introducing me passionately to their own.

Sven, on the other hand, has got me watching TV. On our fourth date he installed a satellite dish in my back yard. On our fifth he gave me a descrambler so I could pick up HBO and Cinemax. "I can't accept this," I said each time. He kissed me hard, then soft, then hard again, mumbling, "Sure you can," and thus it was settled. Our evenings together are spent with peanuts and ESPN, or popcorn and *Starsky and Hutch*, seated side by side on the couch that he has arranged at an angle mathematically calculated to ensure the greatest possible viewing pleasure.

DAD AND I ARE sitting in the living room in opposite chairs, facing one another across the television, listening to the sound of Sven's footsteps on the roof above us. Sven has placed the TV on the floor in the center of the room in the exact spot where Dad's big world globe used to stand. He had to run an extension cord from the TV to the wall in order to reach the outlet, and the thick orange cable snakes menacingly across the polished floor. "It doesn't matter if I move this, does it?" he said earlier, grabbing the beautiful globe by its stem.

"Well," my father said, but Sven had already set the globe down in the corner.

The sofa, two matching chairs, and ottoman that once looked as though they revolved around the globe now more closely resemble a group of stationary satellites, all aimed at the television. The effect of this arrangement on my perspective is startling. For as long as I can remember I have had to lean over in my chair and peer around the globe to see my father, but I am now able to look directly over the top of the TV without obstruction. Dad is drinking water and I'm having milk and Pepsi, a concoction I discovered recently on the syndicated episodes of *Laverne & Shirley*.

"Look," Dad says excitedly, pushing a shoe box across the top of the TV. Inside the box are six daguerreotypes. Four of the pictures show a man, woman, and children. In two, the woman is absent. Upon close examination I notice that it is the same man in every picture, although he is wearing a different suit in each one, holding a different pose, and the expression on his face is varied. In one he looks vaguely amused, in another simply bored, in another he is frowning ferociously. The man is in his fifties, strongly built and handsome. Once, when Mom was alive, we took a trip to Gatlinburg and had our photo taken at an old-fashioned photography studio at the top of Lookout Mountain. We chose antique costumes off a rack—Mom in a severe black dress with a high lace collar and bustle, Dad in a dark suit and bowler hat, me in layers of scratchy crinolines beneath a flouncy yellow number, complete with matching parasol. "Look serious," the photographer commanded. "In the old days you had to sit for five minutes or more waiting for the photo to take, so no one smiled." In the sepia-toned photo, which stands on the dresser in my bedroom, my mother and I manage to appear mean-spirited and grim, but Dad looks as though he's about to break into laughter.

"Is it Cage?" I ask.

"The very man. With the wives and two of the mistresses. All of the daguerreotypes eventually ended up with the second wife, Georgette, who survived all the others. This is Georgette, here's Luda, and Fannie-Mae, and this is Charlotte."

"Each with her own children?"

He nods. "Those who survived infancy." Several of the children are grown and look hardly younger than their mothers. The wives and mistresses themselves appear understandably tired.

"What about the other two mistresses?"

"Elsie and Hanna died in childbirth."

"And Helga?"

Something crashes on the roof, and Sven lets go a long string of curses. My father's gaze travels to the ceiling and lingers there, as if he can look straight through the paint and plywood, insulation and roof frame and shingles, into the mind of this strange creature with whom I share a bed, with whom it is even possible I may choose to share a life. After the cursing subsides Dad says, "Helga remains a mystery. To my knowledge, there are no supporting accounts of her relationship with Cage. All I have to go on are the letter she wrote to him announcing her pregnancy, and the one I'm awaiting, which should arrive from Munich any day."

"Myla, could you hit the power button ?" Sven shouts. I reach for the remote, wishing there were some way I could keep these two loves separate. In letters Cage wrote to his younger brother in Paris, he often spoke of the impossibility of keeping secrets in a place like

Eufala, Alabama, where everyone had ears: "Everyone knows my business. Several of the children go to school together. It has become unbearable." Yet, despite his desire for discretion, Cage sat through six photography sessions with six sets of children, forcing himself to hold the pose while the images took, as if his pride demanded this proof, this irrefutable evidence of his virility.

The television flickers on. There is only a moment of static before the picture appears silently, an exotic place I don't recognize. Dad identifies it immediately. "Saint Petersburg. Your mother and I visited once."

"I don't remember your going there."

"At that time it was called Leningrad. You were just a year old. We left you with Judy. Your mother wanted to see Gatchinsky Palace."

I was twelve when my mother died, thirteen when Dad came across *In A Cold Place* at The Haunted Bookshop in Mobile. It is difficult for me to clearly remember a time before Cage, before so much of my father's energy was focused on that man. I think in some way Cage replaced my mother, a presence to fill the absence she had left, because, unlike Cage, my father is not the kind of man to love many women. "She was it," he told me once, when I was a senior in high school. "She was the one."

Sven shouts down, wanting to know if the picture is clear. I tell him it looks great, and my father, to my surprise, asks me to give it some volume. The program is entirely in Russian. A bald man in a cheap-looking suit sits behind a desk in a small, dimly lit office. A blonde woman is seated in a metal fold-out chair on the other side of the desk. You cannot see the interviewer but you can hear his voice, posing questions alternately to the man and the woman.

"The man being interviewed is a plastic surgeon," Dad explains. "The woman is his patient."

"I didn't know there was a market for cosmetic surgery in Russia."

"Ten years ago there wouldn't have been, but today . . . "

In the flickering light of the television, my father looks older somehow. The firmness has gone out of his neck. His nose looks longer than I remember it, his eyes more sunken. I glimpse the man my father's students must see every day, someone whose life is more than halfway lived, a steady voice of reason imposed on an incomprehensible story.

"Honey, I'm gonna count to three and I want you to turn the set off, then turn it right back on again, you hear me?"

"Got it," I shout, hitting the power button on cue. I wonder if over the years my father has been tempted to judge me by the company I keep, perhaps believing that the intelligent daughter he meant to raise would not love the men I have loved. I wonder if he sometimes wishes that he and my mother had chosen to have a second child, even a third, to balance out the odds. Of Cage's twenty-eight children, twenty-one lived past infancy. Two survived smallpox but were crippled by it, confined to wheelchairs. One was admitted to a sanitarium because of retardation, another for mental illness, and a daughter of one of the mistresses was lost to prostitution. Two died of syphilis as young adults, one was murdered in a land dispute, another jailed for murder. During the war Cage lost his slaves and his inherited fortune, but two of his sons soon reclaimed the plantation and restored the family's wealth. One son became a doctor, one inherited his father's passion for entomology, two daughters took up teaching; there was also a state senator in the bunch. Some simply disappeared into the common malaise of anonymity. Still, Cage bet on the laws of probability and came out on top in the end. My father bet on my mother and me and came out with just me.

The doctor says something that makes the interviewer laugh. The blonde woman nods excitedly and goes into a loud, lengthy monologue.

"What's that about?"

"The doctor is boasting that he has even performed breast augmentation. The woman says she plans to have that done next, after the eyes."

"Thank the Lord some women don't need that sort of thing." Sven has entered the room stealthily, like a man on reconnaissance, and now he stands between me and the television. "Nice piece of work, isn't she?"

My father raises an eyebrow in confusion, caught off guard, unsure if Sven is referring to me or the television. Sven begins channel-surfing and Dad regains his composure, saying, "That was a pretty good program we were watching there." I doubt Dad even notices the slight change in his own vocabulary, the way he automatically shifts into another gear when talking to Sven.

"I bet you speak a little Russian, am I right?" Sven says.

"I know a few words." The truth is Dad is fluent in Spanish, French, German, Italian, and Russian, and also manages to speak passable Cantonese. Never once have I heard him confess to knowing all those languages.

"Now if your picture seems less than perfect, you got to tweak it. To do that you bring up the dish pointing info on the screen, like so, then try several transponders." Sven goes on like this for a while, showing Dad how to move the dish around by remote in order to search for clearer signals or different channels. I can hear the thing clicking and humming above us, occasionally letting out an angry groan, like an alien ship perched on the roof. "At any rate, you got any questions about the dish you call me. I'll do a tune-up on your set in six months."

I am constantly amazed by Sven's faith in the stability of things. He is as certain that he and I will still be a couple six months from now as he is that no man can turn down a satellite dish. That lightning bolt in Little Rock in 1982 taught me one important lesson, which is that nothing is certain or constant, anything can change in an instant. Who knows what happened to Cage's families in the moments after those daguerreotypes were taken. Perhaps Cage believed during each session, while he waited with the photographer's head buried under the black hood of his camera, that he loved the family he was with. Perhaps he discovered that he loved none of them or all of them, or that he had given away too much of himself, or that these six families were not enough and he must create more, and thus his late-in-life affair with Helga von Trask. Perhaps he felt keenly the absence of his seven dead children. The minutes and hours following the photography sessions in the parlors of his mansion in Eufala, and in the less grandiose rooms of his five lesser homes, could have been filled with lovemaking or with fighting. The letters don't tell and we don't know. However Cage perceived his separate lives, history has brought all of his women and children together, the letters bound between the pages of five sturdy volumes, the pictures stored one on top of the other in a shoe box in my father's study. Maybe that is why my father has devoted himself to history, for the sheer solidity of it: our interpretation of any given event may change in time but the facts are cement, the truth doesn't waver, and if some new discovery—for example, a letter from a young girl in Germany revealing a twenty-ninth child—exposes a glitch in what we have accepted as truth, it is not history that has changed, only our knowledge of it.

Sven brings the Russian channel up before announcing that we're leaving. Dad stands and thanks him, and I tell Sven I'll be out soon, then sit for a minute watching Dad watch television. I am feeling a little off balance, confused by this strange new entity spouting foreign words and pictures into Dad's once-pristine space. "You're sweet. You don't have to keep this. He just wanted to give you something."

"No, it's great," Dad says, and I realize he isn't listening to me. All of his attention is focused on the screen, which is showing a before and after picture of the blonde woman. "This woman and her husband used to farm in the country, but as a result of perestroika they were able to realize their dream of opening a small ceramics shop in Saint Petersburg."

While translating, my father is at ease, removed from both the story and me, like a conductor that transports electricity from one point to another. At this moment he exists in the safe in-between where nothing is required of him but to understand and to pass on this understanding. There are moments when you realize something about your parents, and the moments are few and far between but they are everything, because they reveal to you a person beyond the mother or father you have come to know. Now I understand for the first time that my father has always been and will always be a compiler of letters rather than a writer of them, a translator of stories rather than a storyteller.

In the before picture the blonde woman is puffy-eyed and pale, her hair frizzy and unkempt. For the after picture her hair has been styled with sweeping wings and falling waves; you get the feeling that the hairstylist saw old episodes of *Charlie's Angels* decades after the fact, misunderstood the passage of time, and deemed Cheryl Ladd's mass of unruly hair to be fashionable. The woman is also wearing lipstick and blush. To the doctor's credit she does look younger, the flesh beneath her eyes smoothed out, the lids no longer drooping. From a purely aesthetic standpoint she looks rejuvenated, undeniably improved, but there is something almost sinister about the youthfulness of her eyes above the loose skin of her neck and the deep lines around her mouth. It is as if history has been erased from her face, but only partially, so that past and present are unhappily juxtaposed.

My father leans forward to get a closer look. "It's uncanny what modern medicine can do with a laser and a little anesthetic, isn't it?"

"We can at least move it into another room, Mom's old sewing room, maybe. Surely you don't want to keep it here. We can put the globe back. You love that globe."

My father doesn't seem to hear the panic in my voice, lost as he is in the translation. "She says she doesn't want it to end here. She'd like to have her entire face done. She says if she can afford to be transformed entirely into a younger, more beautiful woman, she can

37

SATELLITE

see no reason not to. She believes she has lived with nothing for too long." The picture goes yellow and he bends over the television, looking for knobs to adjust.

"I'm heading out. Call if you want me to come by and take that thing away."

"Bye, sweetie." He stands to give me the obligatory hug, the kiss on the cheek, the quick tug of the ponytail like he has done since I was a kid.

"You coming?" Sven calls from the truck. I go through the kitchen so I can grab a Coke on my way out, then pop my head back in the living room to remind my dad I'm having Judy over for dinner this week and he's invited. He has moved away from the television and is standing in front of the fireplace, staring into the mirror above the mantle. He hated that mirror when my mother put it in. It was one of the few fights they ever had, or at least one of the few I remember. "It makes the room look twice as big," my mother reasoned.

"Not everyone has a face like yours," Dad replied, always able to work a compliment even into an argument, he loved her that much. "Home is supposed to be a haven. The last thing I want to see when I walk into this room is my own ugly face staring back at me." The truth is he had and still has a beautiful face, although I suppose it has never occurred to him to think of himself that way. If my mother were alive I would ask what it was that drew her to him in those first weeks when she was falling in love, months before marriage, long before me, years before she sat on the wrong end of a bench in Little Rock, Arkansas, her dark, broad face and long black hair inviting electricity—back when my grandparents still believed she might end up with a man of medicine, someone wealthy and ambitious who would make for her an exceptional life. I would ask her if, like Sven, like Cage, my father's was once the kind of face that would make a woman think she could change her ways for him, forgiving bad manners and infidelity, disappointing her family and even disappointing something in herself, just for the beauty of him.

My father squints his eyes and relaxes them, pokes at the loose flesh with his fingers, forms a V with middle and index finger and drags at the bags beneath his eyes. He frowns, then mumbles something to himself so quietly I cannot make out the words. He flattens the skin beneath his chin with the back of his hand, then places his palms on either side of his face and tugs the skin toward his hairline. His mouth widens, the corners of his eyes stretch ghoulishly, the skin looks thin enough to break. I imagine one day I will walk into this house and find him in his chair in front of the television, his face bruised by a surgeon's hands, the skin stretched to unnatural proportions.

Outside Sven is fidgeting, growing impatient; in the quiet neighborhoods of Fayetteville this fine Saturday, customers stand on their porches and wait for him. Somewhere a father walks inside and dusts the screen of the television set. He calls his family into the living room, where they will fight over the most comfortable chairs, then wait with snacks and fizzy drinks for the man with the satellite dish. They know that he is coming, they have all gathered around to greet him, Sven believes this in his heart.

Through the rear window of Sven's truck, I can see the big white dish on Dad's roof. The monster moves slowly back and forth, its antenna poised like a lightning rod, searching the Arkansas sky for signals beamed down from space.

Slacabamorinico

*T*he Sunday before Fat Tuesday in the port city of Mobile, revelers dance on Joe Cain's grave in the Church Street cemetery. In 1866, Joe Cain rode through the streets of Mobile on the back of a coal wagon, dressed as Slacabamorinico, the legendary Chickasaw chief. Joe Cain and his crew made a general ruckus. An old mule plodded along before them. "Take this," Joe said to the Union troops who occupied the city.

Those who dance on Joe Cain's grave are quick to tell you it all started here, in the streets of Mobile in eighteen and sixty-six. They christen the headstone with beer bottles, water the grass around his grave with straight bourbon and piss. Men dress in women's clothing. Women stand on shifting balconies of old French hotels, lift their shirts for passing floats, bare their breasts to the kindly spirit of Joe Cain. Joe Cain's bones dance a knock-kneed lay-down kind of dance at the sight of the bare-chested happy women. On Joe Cain's grave, teenaged boys get laid for the first time, and the heat of their quick love seeps down into the fertile earth. Slacabamorinico himself is rumored to be buried somewhere on the outskirts of Mobile County, in an unmarked grave near an abandoned skating rink.

The year before Hurricane Frederick, our father took Darlene and Celia and me to the Crew of Columbus parade. We clambered to catch plastic necklaces and chocolate doubloons, felt the crowd crushing forward as we sang the Moon Pie chant. A big man in overalls nearly knocked me over when he reached out to catch a shower of Jolly Ranchers. He stepped on my foot and sloshed beer on my shirt. On the way home I ate twenty-six Now & Laters and vomited out the window of our Galaxy 500.

When we got home our mother was waiting at the front door. "You smell like beer!" she said, dragging me inside. I felt grown up and slightly sinful, like the prodigal child come home. My mother was so angry she locked my father out of the house. Late into the evening he paid penance for the debauchery we had witnessed, sitting on the doorstep staring out at the street.

Years later I would learn of the infamous Cowbellions, with their rakes and hoes and cowbells, their bovine inclinations, their triumphant march through the streets of Mobile decades before the war. Drunk on whiskey and New Year, they rang their bells and clanged their rakes until the whole city awoke. In their hearts that night there was no inkling of the coming War of Northern Aggression, no thought of the slaves who peered in disbelief from the dim windows of their shanties. Mobilians don't know that the party has long since ended, clinging hardheadedly to the notion that the Confederates won the war.

The

Last

Bad

Thing

I saw him at Sabrina's on Fourteenth Street. I left without speaking to him and for the next two days hated myself for allowing him to pass so quietly through my life. When I returned two nights later he was there, wearing the same vest, holding the same stance. I gave him my address. He wrote his name with the nub of a pencil on someone else's business card. By the time I left New York City and headed home to Mobile, the "I" in Ivan had already begun to wear off.

Since then, he has been writing me. In his first letter, Ivan explained that he was a math teacher at Rye Country Day School, but his National Guard unit had been called up for duty in the Gulf, and the address on the business card would no longer be valid. The address I have now begins with the letters S.P.C., followed by Ivan's social security number, followed by more words and numbers I can't pronounce, and all I can deduce is that he is stationed thousands of miles away.

I am the only person he has ever met from Alabama. In my letters, I try to explain what it is like: *The beaches to the south justify this state's existence. They make up for our governor, for Mobile politics. The dog-woods and azaleas make a pretty good case for us too. I have been to the California coast and it's much more menacing than ours. There is such a sense of spaciousness here, of temporal ease.*

Here is what he tells me. It is Ramadan. Many times a day the people come out of their homes—the men and boys white-robed, the women cloaked in black—and bow toward Mecca. From their apartments the American soldiers can hear them chanting and wailing. Everything white, and the sound of all those voices, and inside their rooms the Americans read love letters and play Nintendo.

My own letters shy away from any reference to us, the thing we might become. It's too soon to turn us into a full-blown subject, with our own history and mutual future, a code only we can decipher. Within the white envelopes that are delivered to him each Monday he finds only the beginnings of stories, incomplete lists, slim sugges-tions of the truth. *What moves me: the fog rolling over the bay in those pictures of San Francisco, chocolate, a man alone in a restaurant reading his newspaper intently. The boy in my neighborhood who watched me this afternoon as I walked by.*

He was twelve or thirteen and had just set a sprinkler on his lawn. He stood by his door, watching. The shower caught me as I passed. I admired him for not looking away when I saw him, for being on that edge where he is deciding how he will live his life. I smiled at him and thought of the boys I knew when I was his age. Of Jamie, who gave me my first kiss.

I was fourteen. I was spending the night with my friend Angel Brady in the big house on Delancey Street, where she lived with her aunt and uncle after her parents died. Unlike her parents, Angel's aunt and uncle never got religion, and as a result they let us do as we pleased. I didn't tell my own parents that Jamie would be there—Jamie who was eighteen and had introduced himself to me and Angel at a youth evangelism conference in Lookout Mountain, Tennessee. He claimed to be Canadian, said he spoke impeccable French. "I may not look muscular, but I have wiry strength," he said, and broke a broomstick over his knee to prove it. Jamie and I watched the 1984 Olympics on TV, nestled on the couch like lovers who had been together for years. That was the year Mary Lou Retton ran off with two gold medals. If you were an American girl and your parents had said dream big, you wanted to be Mary Lou. She represented the best of what a girl could be. Mary Lou had just performed a perfect dismount, her chalked feet slapping solidly against the mat, when Jamie pressed his hand against my neck, turned my face in his direction. His tongue inside the warm spaces of my mouth, the heat of his breath, a quiet fear, something inside me pushing outward. Quickly he lifted my shirt and touched his fingers to my breast. I imagined tiny slivers of glass pricking my skin.

The next morning Jamie kissed me by the window as my father's green Chevrolet pulled into Angel's driveway. I am certain my father saw us. On the way home, my mind was on the thing that was between us now, my father and me, and I didn't know what I would say to him about the boy in the window. When he said, "You have to listen," I braced myself for the lecture. But he didn't mention Jamie. He turned the windshield wipers on, despite the fact that it wasn't raining, turned them off again, and said, "Mr. Dupree is dead." I didn't say a word as he told me how it happened. A few minutes later, we arrived safely home. My mother was waiting with breakfast, scrambled eggs and grits and bacon.

Mr. Dupree was a close friend of the family, unmarried and childless, who had been coming to my birthday parties for as long as I could remember. Seven years before, on the day my mother went to the hospital to have Baby, Darlene and Celia and I had walked to the curb outside Greystone Christian School to find Mr. Dupree waiting there for us. He took us to Dairy Queen, bought us peanut-butter parfaits, and told us the news: the baby was a girl, there were slight but not serious complications, and we would be spending the night with him while our parents were at the hospital.

Before that day, we had never been to Mr. Dupree's house; he had always come to us. At our birthday parties he never failed to bring gifts that kept our interest long after we had forgotten the others; for my seventh birthday he had given me a Fischer Price Chemistry Set to mix my own eye shadows and blushes, my own lipstick and perfume. Because of his understanding of the finer points of girlhood, and because of his quiet demeanor, I always considered him to be the most gentle of my parents' friends. So I was shocked when he opened the double front doors of his home that afternoon and I saw that the furniture in his living room was draped in animal furs, the walls covered with antlers and skins. Everywhere I looked I met the flat eyes of something dead, some animal he had shot and stuffed. For dinner he served deer meat. It was salty and tough, like no meat I had ever tasted.

Mr. Dupree kept us up well into the night, long past our nine o'clock bedtime. He ran his womanly fingers over the nostrils and ears and antlers of animals that stared back at us with glassy eyes, and as he touched the big, dead beasts he told the story of each conquest. He described opening day of hunting season in Bucksnort, Tennessee, a safari in the Sahara, ten days in the Alaskan wilderness. As he spoke I thought of my mother's swollen belly, how it would be smaller now, and how when I laid my head against her stomach I would no longer feel the baby moving. I thought of the infant girl I would go home to, and I felt something grown-up stirring inside me; suddenly I felt very sure and brave.

"I guess I've been just about everywhere," Mr. Dupree said before finally dismissing us for bed. "I guess I've killed just about every kind of creature." This new information about Mr. Dupree did not frighten me; it only made me love him more, and my affection for him grew as I entered adolescence. His was a world so unlike our own, full of mystery and danger.

My father told me that a drunk driver had hit Mr. Dupree head on while he was driving home late from work. It occurred to me that this had happened while I was watching the Olympics, holding hands with a guy I hardly knew. Mr. Dupree's Jeep landed upside down in a ditch. The picture that came to me, that day and for years after, was an image of four tires turned up to the sky, so still beneath the moon, and underneath the tires, somewhere down below, the body of the man we had known.

For years I felt responsible for Mr. Dupree's death. It is not unusual for Baptist children to feel this way. Whenever something terrible happens to someone you love, you automatically think of the last bad thing you did and wonder if it is somehow connected to the tragedy. And you wonder when a friend or a cousin will do something equally bad, something unspeakable, and exactly when it will come back to you in the form of disease or disaster.

Pardon me for talking about the weather, but it's relevant. In your letters you say the nights are cold, but I see the pictures on television and I can't imagine that place could ever be anything short of scorching. Here it is tempting eighty. The driveway has already begun its annual upheaval. The asphalt softens, breaks against the pressure of the giant mushrooms that push their way through like nobody's business; the mushrooms have thick, wide caps, three to four inches in diameter. The weeds behind the house have overtaken the old oak tree, and a group of boys who call themselves the Gladiators have commandeered the pump-house the neighborhood kids use for a fort. I guess it all comes down to who is the strongest.

ANGEL AND I met in elementary school. Angel was Pentecostal, but her parents sent her to Greystone because there were no Pentecostal schools in Fairhope or Mobile, and Greystone's radical brand of

Baptist was the closest they could come to the strict rules of their own faith. In kindergarten, our sleeping mats were right next to each other. Mine was red, hers blue. We had just learned the alphabet. We printed our names on the mats with Magic Markers in thick, ungraceful letters, claiming them as our own. The girls slept on one side of the room, the boys on the other. The boys' sleeping mats were beside the windows. They could lie on their backs, eyes open, looking out at everything green. I envied this view. I wanted to know who was walking in the courtyard, what the sun was doing in the sky.

Angel would never go to sleep at nap time. She stayed awake, lying on her side, trying to get me to talk to her. "I'm scared, Gracie," she would whisper. "Don't go to sleep." So I would whisper back to her, lying in the shadows, and I don't remember what we talked about but I know it was delicious to be such intimate friends, to talk so quietly, knowing the danger. When Mrs. Blade heard us she would call us up to the front of the room and slap our wrists with a plastic ruler.

We went to chapel every morning and prayed the way they taught us, rhymed prayers that made no sense. We wore navy jumpers with navy button-downs underneath, navy kneesocks and saddle shoes. Once a month we had hem check; we never knew when it was coming. All the girls lined up in front of the room, kneeling. Mrs. Blade went down the row with a measuring tape and made sure our hems touched the floor. Twice in one year, my dress was too short. I lined up single file with the other girls whose uniforms exposed some downy slice of leg, and we marched to the office. Then Coach Tipton took us into the office one by one, and we held down the backs of our skirts while he gave us three good whops with the paddling board. Then, in your navy jumper and kneesocks, you never thought to question any of it.

IN MOBILE *it has been raining for weeks now, but it doesn't thunder.*

I send these letters to Ivan, and I tell him only the barest and safest details of my life. His letters to me are brief, littered with numerical references: 164 cases of sanitary napkins buried in the sand because things are coming to an end and there is no way his unit can bring home all the supplies they've accumulated; 32 days since the war ended and no telling when he'll get to come home; 16 weeks since he spotted me sitting alone in a corner booth at Sabrina's; 7 days of quiet rain outside his apartment building in Al Khubar; 129 high school math students back in Rye, New York, awaiting his return. He says that numbers are his strong suit and words never add up right. I will have to imagine the rest.

Looking out my window at the rain that doesn't stop, I know this is how it is in that country—deep, thunderless rains. There, the orange earth whips up in clouds and comes at you like a tornado, until the rain comes and soothes the rage. Here, the rain hits the skylight like pebbles, beats the grass with an incessant thud, hammers the house into the soft earth. It is something to think about, the orange earth rising in a fury of particles, rising and subsiding in the place where everything but the earth is white. The apartment buildings are white. Americans there for the war sunbathe on top of them when there is nothing else to do. There is often nothing else to do. Inside, just Nintendo, and books and magazines sent from home, letters from students who beg, "Come home soooon! Why are they keeping you there?"

TWO MONTHS ago I graduated from college. I have moved in with my family while I decide what to do with my life. It's nice being home, settling into the old routines. In this house I become a child again.

We have just had our evening meal, sitting around the big, rectangular table like the family that we are. We held hands and said the blessing. "Dear God, thank you for our food, thank you for everything you have given us, please take care of Grandmother and Aunt Lucy and everyone we love, in Jesus' name we pray, Amen." I say the entire prayer in one breath. I have been repeating the same prayer since I was six.

Everyone has his or her turn to pray. Mostly "her," because the only "he" is our father. He is outnumbered. His prayer always begins, "Lord, bless this food that we are about to eat." Each of us has one prayer that we have been repeating for years at the dinner table. Except Baby. She's fifteen. She gets creative. Sometimes she says, "Dear God, please help me not to get fat, since Mom put a ton of butter in these beans." I think we are all a bit envious of the way she talks to God.

There are 500 churches in the city of Mobile. 500. I have only been to 3 of them.

Just lately we have begun fragmenting. I told my family I'm moving to New York, but I don't tell them what Ivan wrote in his last letter: *27 detached fingers found at the camp where 9 Americans died from friendly fire. 6 months since I got here. Yesterday I counted 31 letters from you. 1 bedroom in my apartment in Rye. Will you come to New York?* In reply I sent him a postcard bearing a picture of Dauphin Island taken before the big hurricane of '79. In the picture small houses stand on stilts close to the shoreline. There are no people, only white beach and run-down houses, and an old fishing boat half-buried in the sand. *2 suitcases*, I wrote. *26 books I can't leave behind. Are you sure you have room?*

Darlene left a few years ago with a beautiful girl named Beth. They drove Beth's beat-up El Camino all the way to Bandera, Texas. Whenever one of us mentions Beth, my mother says, "Darlene's confused. She'll come around." But she doesn't come around, and we are not allowed to call her, so I buy phone cards at the K&B on Hillcrest and dial her number from the pay phone. "Hey hot shot," Beth says whenever she answers the phone, and I think of her standing in our driveway on the day she took Darlene, looking brazen and bad-tempered in the world's greatest pants.

Celia graduated from Mobile College last year and has been living at home, biding her time until life began to happen. Now she plans to marry and move to Atlanta. She already has a wedding date at Bay View Baptist Church. Baby is going to be a missionary, live in the jungle, and eat roots and berries. She also would like a house by the ocean and a mountain chalet. "You can't buy anything on a missionary's salary," I tell her.

Mother is proud of her, but worried. She sits at the table and listens to our plans, drinks her coffee black. She traces the scars on the Formica tabletop with her fingers. There was a time, when the table was new, that she guarded it like her own children. She kept it safe from our childhood scissors and markers, protected it with place mats when we ate. For my mother, things have always been hard to come by. I think she is resigned now to their inevitable disintegration, to the way her children, unthinking, destroy the things she has acquired. She traces the scars we have made, and I notice her hands are getting older. The veins are thick, bulky. I look at them and think how they are pumping life through her body. She used to be an RN and got strong from squeezing the little black rubber bulbs on the ends of the blood pressure cuffs. When I was small I used to get her to take my blood pressure. I remember the wide band around my arm that fastened with a Velcro strip, the way it went on loose and then she started working that rubber pump, and the band got fat with air around my arm, tingling. My mother no longer nurses, she hasn't touched a blood pressure pump in years, but even now she can open any jar you give her. She holds the jar tight under her left arm, and with her right hand gives the lid an unholy twist. She is beautiful, with hazel eyes that none of us got. My father's eyes are brown.

Some days my mother seems like the happiest person on earth, like when she jiggles her hips and cups my face in her hands and sings, "You're still my little baby, even if you're going off to New York to live with all the crazies." Sometimes this fact crosses my mind and I don't know what to do with it: we are all leaving her.

THE LAST BAD THING

WITH THE LETTERS, Ivan sends rolls of film that he asks me to develop. In the one-hour Photomat, the man behind the counter issues orders to his wife, who is small and wears a yellow smock. I recognize them from my parents' church. He's a deacon; she teaches children's choir. They have the look of doomed religion about them, the resigned faces of people who understand they have been pressed eternally into the service of the church.

"Our son didn't get to go," the woman says, sliding the envelope across the counter. "He's stuck in Fort Rucker."

Driving home, I think of the sealed envelope beside me on the seat, the images concealed there. I expect to see pictures of soldiers horsing around in exotic shops, playing backgammon inside the white rooms of their apartment buildings. In my bedroom of my old house, I open the envelope, remove the glossy photos from their plastic sleeve, lean back against the pillow. The walls of my bedroom disappear and I enter this foreign landscape. For a moment I can see him there:

He is walking. It is dusk. The road from Kuwait. Telephone lines slope from pole to pole, cable sure in the clear sky. Nothing breathes beside the cleared road. The buses rest on their sides, windows gone in February's dry heat. The bodies have been covered, the charred messes swept over with sand. The desert valley, stunned by death, sinks below the shadows of sand hills at dusk. The tanks lie side to side like dominoes. He overturns a fender with his boot and finds an arm in its brown sleeve, intact, leaving its isolated imprint in the sand.

This is the truth. The solid things remain: a looted yellow tricycle with one twisted wheel, small refrigerators, two brown throw pillows gathering grit. He reaches destruction's end, leaves the stolen goods behind—the diaries, the missile scraps with their Magic Marker dedications. He is stunned at dusk by the ease of death, the way a gutted truck, upturned, lifts its unharmed tires toward the sky. There are no rivers, no cool mirages.

THERE IS MORE to tell about Angel. When I was a junior in high school she was raped behind Dreamland Skating Rink, right across the road from Bay Street Baptist Church. The church is huge and white, with a steeple so high it seems as though it is punching a hole in the sky. When I was a child the steeple terrified me, the way it reached so high above the telephone lines and traffic lights, so high above the skating rink. Everything around the church looked insignificant in comparison. On clear nights when the moon shone brightly, the steeple cast its long, pointed shadow over the parking lot and out into the bay. The girls going into the skating rink, in their tight jeans and soft, pastel-colored sweaters, made a game of walking straight down the middle of the shadow.

The skating rink is a rectangular building with aluminum siding, alternating yellow and blue panels. I used to go there with Celia on weekends. I stopped going the summer before ninth grade. So did most of my friends. But not Angel. The rape happened in February of our junior year. *February is the coldest month in Mobile. Everyone freezes because no one owns winter coats, just denim jackets and windbreakers. The winter always takes us by surprise. We are prepared here for hurricanes and tornadoes, thunderstorms so violent they rip the limbs from big oak trees—but not for cold.* Angel was probably chilled to the bone the night she went behind the skating rink to smoke with one of the referees. He knocked her around with his fists before he did it, slammed her head against the aluminum siding. He got her pregnant. I was the one who convinced her not to have the baby. I remember waiting for her in the lobby of the clinic. The walls were painted a milky green.

Sometimes, still, I see the tires of Mr. Dupree's Jeep, turning, upturned in the night, beside the black road. No one has found him yet. The other driver goes on, swerves his way into the darkness. The wheels turn, and slow, and turn no more. The hubcaps, in the moonlight, cast a metallic glow.

A cat emerges from the woods across the road, ascends the Jeep, stands upon a tire. He arches momentarily, hisses, then settles, declaring it home. And underneath it all: Mr. Dupree, in his silent contortion, unfound.

AMERICANS THERE for the war are wondering when they will get to come home. They sign their names on a piece of white paper that is stuck to a clipboard. The clipboard has a chewed, army-issue pencil tied to it with string. After signing, they are allowed to take the video camera with them. They have to return it in four hours, but that is enough time to ride around Al Khubar in the back of an army truck. They make wide turns, and the natives in their white cars smile and wave their white-sleeved arms at the Americans.

There is a tall American with dark hair whose fatigues are loose from the weight he has lost on his six-month diet of Ramen noodles and saltines. He points to the sign of the Phuk-Et Restaurant and makes crude, quiet jokes about the name. It is not the Ivan I thought I knew, the one I was attracted to that first night at Sabrina's. I wonder if in so short a time this place has changed him. There is laughter in the background, from behind the camera.

A woman in a long black robe crosses the street, slowly and with her head bowed. Her hair and face are covered, her wrists and ankles. She walks behind a man in his white robe and a child, a boy, who smiles and waves at the Americans. Soon this man and this boy and this woman in her life-long mourners' clothes will bow toward Mecca. They will sing-chant a prayer, high-pitched and broken, and it will remind you of charred arms and sand-dune graves, but it will be a prayer of praise, not suffering. The woman will hold the edges of her black robe. The boy and the man will be yards away, facing the same direction, their white robes bright in the sun. The child will think of his mother and look to her, and see her bent and black and formless.

SOMETIMES AT night when I lie awake, my mother comes into my room and sits on the edge of my bed. She tucks one foot underneath her, wraps her arms around a pillow. Her face is shiny from night cream. She surveys the scars I have made on the walls of my bedroom where I have tacked up stark and startling photographs, strange prints. In one of the paintings, a woman bends gauntly over an ironing board, her black hair hanging toward her hands.

"You should go to New York with me," I say, and mean it. I would like to have her with me, a beautiful Southern woman in that strange and alien place. When Ivan returns, I would like for him to meet her. She says New York is dangerous. I say Mobile is dangerous too. I tell her the water in our hometown will give her cancer. I tell her everything nasty from the whole country floats down to Mobile Bay. I tell her that these things I am saying are true, that I learned them in college.

Even as I try to persuade her, I know that my mother will never leave this place. I am beginning to understand why. She is not in love with the city itself, but with the house where her children grew up. The children that she knew and are gone now, somehow inhabit these beloved rooms. In some way they are here, and they are not elsewhere. She is the only one in the world who truly knows these children. We, changed, do not know them. Our father does not know them.

I think of Ivan in the place where he is now, the place it seems he will always be, and I wonder what sounds may reach him. Does he still hear the long, enraptured wail of Ramadan? In my dreams I am there, I see him but he is far away. I keep company with the voices, they are trapped with me beneath the black cloaks; their presence is physical, thick as oil. I do not want to be in this strange place, where the women cast their impassioned prayers toward Mecca. They are shadows, bent and black, against the whitest landscape.

Ramadan. I wake with the word on my lips. My body feels bloated and gone—a sent, lost prayer, a thing unanswered.

I admire you for your focus, for knowing what you want. Perhaps you are like this because of your affinity for numbers. Everything for you is so

THE LAST BAD THING

defined. Everything has set parameters. I wonder if we will ever master our differences, make sense of what separates us.

I don't tell him that two cats are going at it on the driveway. With cats it is always a struggle, always like rape. I want to pull the male cat off the female, but there are some things you cannot interfere with; a certain order must be maintained.

In Ivan's letters he writes of alien things, of theorems and theories, of the way my shoulders, bared to the cold, moved him those two nights last winter. He speaks of the angles my body makes, as if my body were a definitive structure, a mathematical thing. I want to say to him, *Numbers will not save you.* I want to say to him, *They will not save the world.* But I choose my words too carefully. I tell him such small things.

Sixteen

*B*aby wears shoes that make her six feet tall. She breaks the hearts of unsuspecting boys on a daily basis. Recently she broke the heart of a boy named Gordo. Gordo has an Australian accent, although he has lived his entire short life in Mobile, Alabama. After having his heart broken by my little sister, Gordo wrote a song about her. Now every Saturday night his band plays the song at the Culture Shock downtown, not forty yards from the Church Street cemetery, where under the warm wet earth Joe Cain's joyous knees are knocking. When the band plays the song, all the girls cast jealous glances Baby's way. When Baby dances, she sways her head like Bob Dylan, rocks her shoulders, pretends her arms are branches. Her legs stand still as a tree trunk. When Baby dances, her big shoes grow roots. Sixteen is all that matters.

And then: Baby grows up and meets a man named Jake whose line of work is suspicious. Jake has a bank account and a basement and a box filled with items the names of which confound me. Buz-divan, for example. Ring gag. In the letters she sends from Knox-ville, Tennessee, where this man has taken her, Baby tells me little things about her life that I'd be better off not knowing. In retrospect I see that my advice to her was poor, that I did her a great disservice by always telling the truth.

"Describe it in one word," she used to say, meaning sex, and I would reply in all honesty and with far too much enthusiasm, "Grand!" Perhaps she would have been wiser to seek advice from Celia and Darlene. Celia is happily married to a man with whole-some ways. Darlene would have said, "It's fabulous, as long as you find the right girl."

Now I fear Baby has taken it too far. She has become a housewife who does the sort of things one learns about on late-night television, the sort of things housewives are known for far and wide.

"Gracie, am I a housewife?" she asks one afternoon over the tele-phone.

"No," I say, learning to lie. She breathes a sigh of great relief, as if by proclaiming it I can make it true.

Something is going on in the background, the details of which elude me. "Perhaps the moccasins?" I hear someone say. It is not the voice of her husband.

Propaganda

*T*wice in my life I have taken money for sex. The first time didn't count because it was my husband Jake who paid me. He gave me six dollars in quarters, which I used up at the Laundromat. He was wearing pajamas decorated with cowboy hats and cowboy boots and chaps and spurs and horses. We made love on top of Indians and bonfires, rendered intricately in browns and rusty reds on the flannel sheets. At one point, he put his hand against his mouth and yelled, "Owa! Owa! Owa!" like an Indian in an old western.

I said, "No, no. That's not right. You're supposed to be the cowboy. Look! My hair is in braids. I'm wearing moccasins. Isn't it obvious?"

He said, "Sometimes I get carried away, Baby. I just forget." "Baby" is not necessarily an affectionate term. It's the name my sisters pinned on me when I was too young to protest. By the time I started kindergarten I wouldn't answer to anything else.

"You shouldn't forget," I said. "You have the gun. Indians didn't have guns, doofus, only cowboys."

I don't like him having a gun. We have argued about it often. But Jake is required by his job to keep the gun near him at all times. Thus its nocturnal placement on the small wooden table beside the bed, the table that was passed down to me by my great aunt the pacifist, who served as a WAC in World War II. Eleven and a half months ago, before Jake left for his latest stint in Urbistan, he had me bent over the foot of the bed and was spanking my bottom with enthusiasm when my blindfold slipped and I caught sight of the gun, lying there in its black leather holster. I stood and covered myself with a pillow.

"I can't do this," I said. "It doesn't feel right, playing S&M games in the presence of her table, with the added insult of your gun." I walked over to the table, picked up the gun, pointed in his direction and said, "If you don't get rid of this thing, I'm going to shoot you."

Jake just sat on the edge of the bed, took off his socks and said, "What do you want me to do? Quit my job?" His socks had little holes where the toenails had rubbed through.

"I bet if I told them a few things."

A weak threat. I would never tell. Just your garden-variety sex games. Cowboys and Indians. Lipstick, garters, and red high heeled shoes in special sizes to fit a man of stature. Motorcycle helmets and dangerous boots and long whips with cool leather fringe. It probably wouldn't matter anyway. Ever since the organization's venerable founder died in the sixties, they don't care so much about private lives. There are only two rules anymore that really count: one, don't commit adultery, and two, don't sleep with an informant. When Jake told me this rule, I asked, "What would happen if your wife sleeps with one of your informants?"

"I don't know. The handbook doesn't address that issue. Still, I'm sure they would advise against it."

Which is why the informant and I have never slept together. We just watch each other—night after night, day after day—rarely speaking, never discussing the thing that has grown up between us.

ONCE, SITTING at the top step of the staircase that leads from my apartment to his, the informant said, "I am not your mother or your lover or your friend. I am just this man who watches you undress."

I walked to the door that separates our apartments and said, "But I'm not undressing. It's just a fantasy of yours."

This is one of only two conversations we have ever had.

The door at the bottom of the staircase was added a few years ago to divide the house into apartments. It is not a door meant for entering and leaving; it has been nailed shut and locked with a dead bolt to which no one has the key. The upper half of the door is a panel of etched glass enclosed in a white wooden frame. Neither of us has covered it with a curtain. This way we can see each other, as long as he is in his stairwell or I am in my living room. I wear thin white skirts made of gauze through which he can see anything he wants to see. Sometimes I might wear two towels, one wrapped around my waist and the other around my wet head, after my cool bath in the evening. Cool because hot water prematurely ages the skin. I am twenty-four and painfully aware of my body's passage through time. A single, straight line has appeared on my forehead.

"Mark my word," I say to my sister Grace one afternoon in August, toward the end of my twenty-fourth year of living. "I am growing old."

The informant and I live in Knoxville, Tennessee, in the big yellow house on Amelia Street. He inhabits the top floor. The bottom belongs to me and my husband, although Jake has never actually lived here; he left for Urbistan a week after we moved in.

The man upstairs is from Urbistan's capital, Urada. A sizable Urbistanian community has developed in Knoxville during the past five years, across the railroad tracks just past the Old City. The man upstairs slips sealed envelopes beneath the door with "Cowboy" scribbled on them. My husband got that name from his colleagues because he grew up in South Dakota and had dreams of cattle rop-ing. When he says, "When I was a kid, I dreamed of being a cowboy," he means it for the truth. Three generations before him were cow-boys, but things went bad in the cattle industry when he was still a toddler. Instead of becoming a cowboy he went to college and stud-ied Eastern European languages, then went to law school. After that he put in his bid for government work. It took them two-and-a-half years to hire him. After all was said and done he realized it wasn't the job he wanted, but he had invested too much time. His family no longer owned cattle. His father was dead.

I accept Jake's explanation of his chosen profession just as I accept it every time word comes down from the office that we have to move to a different house, a different neighborhood. Jake tells me that most of his colleagues live somewhat normal lives, that their families are relatively unaffected by the job. With us, it's different. Jake has gotten into this thing so deep, the rules for us have changed. Faith-fully I have lived the past three years of my life in accordance with the organization's decree. I never know the details, and I don't want to.

I HAVE ALWAYS liked the names of women. A woman's name is a good place to put a house. Before Amelia Street, we lived at 2101 Nadine Drive, and before that, 180 Linda Jo Place. Three weeks ago I received a message from Jake's office that it was time to relocate again, "just as a precaution." So I have chosen a small blue house on Lillian Road, a house with a porch that faces a cemetery where no one I know is buried.

When I was a child in Alabama, my father developed subdivisions and built homes. I made lists of names he should give to the streets of the subdivisions. I named them after my older sisters, Grace and Celia and Darlene, and after my Great Aunt Juliana, whose table was passed down to me. Esmerelda Drive also made my list. Endora

Circle. Samantha Street. These were the names of witches on TV, women who could alter history with a snap of their fingers or a twitch of their noses. They could clean their houses in this manner, or turn a person into a billy goat, or transport themselves to the south of France, or make a man love them with an all-cosuming love. I liked biblical names as well: Naomi Court, Ruth Place, Mary and Martha Circle, Rahab Drive.

Rahab, in real life, was a giant prostitute who lived in the city of Jericho. She lowered two Israelite spies out her window in a basket, over the city walls, to the safety of Joshua's army that awaited word below. Joshua's army marched seven times around the walls of Jericho, shouting and clanging symbols. On the seventh revolution the walls crumbled. The army rushed in and killed with sword every living thing, including women and children. Because of her act of betrayal Rahab was saved. I imagine the streets all full of blood, and Rahab and her family safe within that home, her sheets still stained with the sperm of the Israelite spies, the rope that held the giant basket still dangling from the window.

FOR A WHILE I wrote to Jake care of the American embassy in Urada, but he only wrote back a couple of times. He says staying in touch makes it dangerous for me. He says we can't be too careful. I haven't heard from him in four months. He wants me to believe that this lack of communication is simply a hazard of the job, but at the occasional company function, to which I am always invited, the other spouses look at me with pity.

"How long?" Elizabeth Ernest said at the Easter egg hunt a month ago this Saturday. I mark my calendar by holidays; none escape my notice. The holidays named after groundhogs and presidents, martyrs and saints and saviors, hold equal weight with me. I went to the Easter egg hunt, despite the fact that I have no children. I made a basket of plastic eggs, each filled with Susan B. Anthony dollars I collected back in high school. The children were thrilled to find my eggs. Several fights broke out over my eggs. Sally Mitchum's girl had eight stitches in her knee after being hit with a baseball bat.

"Four months?" Elizabeth said, rearranging the pink plastic grass in her child's Easter basket. "That seems odd. Well, I'm sure there's a reason."

Sometimes late at night the telephone will ring, and I will believe in my half-sleep that it is Jake calling to tell me he's coming home. When I answer, it is a man's voice I hear, but not my husband's.

"Ankle," the man says. "Belly button. Breasts." He is only calling to recite the names of women's body parts. Each time he calls, he becomes bolder, adds a more intimate word. He says the words with reverence, as though he is reciting lines from the Bible. I always let the man hang up first. I fall back to sleep and dream of my husband, of his hands touching each part the caller has named.

Sometimes, going about my business, I run into people I used to know. Invariably they ask about my husband. "He's out of the country," I say. "You know, business." They look at me with sympathy, as if they know some secret, as if there is something they aren't telling me. Sometimes it seems that everyone around me is in on the government's paycheck, that all of them have been pressed into service to ensure the preservation of this delicate ruse—the illusion of my marriage to a man whom I don't see or talk to.

I imagine that every now and then Jake meets a dark-haired woman who asks him about his wife. He does not deny my existence, my significance in his life, the importance of a soul-mate. The fact that he is married only makes him more attractive, mysterious, tragic.

"It must be difficult to be away from her," the woman says. She fingers the hem of her long skirt, relaxes her shoulders, offers him tea. "It is difficult to be only."

"Alone," Jake says gently. "The word is alone, not only."

I can see him bowing his head briefly, then leaning in to kiss her. Perhaps in the moment before their lips touch he remembers me, the little mole above my upper lip, the tiny scar winding into my hairline. Perhaps he recalls my blue satin dress with the safety pin hidden beneath the strap, or his brown shoes with the upcurled tongues that stand at the foot of our bed.

ONCE, SITTING in the leopard print chair in the living room, I looked up to see the informant's face pressed against the window of our shared door. At first I wasn't sure he was there at all, because I was sitting in the pool of light cast by my reading lamp and there was no light in his apartment. My vision somehow adjusted to the darkness of the stairwell, and I saw that it wasn't only his face that was pressed against the window, but his entire body. His hips were moving slightly against the glass.

I was reading a collection of stories titled *Wake Up, It's Time to Go to Sleep!* by the Urbistanian writer Jiri Kajane. I read it because I wanted to know about this strange country that had become, so completely, my husband's life, a country I had never visited, the place that filled his days and nights and had been his obsession for as long as I had known him. I placed the book face down on my knee and watched the informant watching me. He paused for a moment, then resumed the slow motion of his hips against the glass. Seconds later his movement quickened. Then he shuddered and was still.

"What are you doing?" My words came out as a shout. "Please tell me exactly what it is that you are doing."

"You're beautiful." The way he said it struck me as so pathetic and sincere, so devoid of design or malice, that I could think of no reply.

"Thank you," I said. This was the second and last conversation we ever had. On this evening I was wearing gray sweatpants and Jake's thick black cardigan, not out of modesty but because it was cold. Even now, when I think of that night, I cannot imagine what it was about me that compelled the man upstairs to press his body against the door, what he could have seen in me. Time and again he had watched me moving quietly through my living room, draped flimsily in clothes that I chose with our silent, symbiotic relationship in mind. And he had never so much as pressed a foot forward on the stairwell to come near me. Why did he choose this night, when I was fully covered? Why, this night, did I provoke him? Did I elicit some nostalgia for the drab fabrics of his homeland? Did I recall a woman he once knew?

SINCE JAKE LEFT, a petite blonde woman named Hanna has been coming to my door every Friday just as dark sets in. Each time, I attempt to lure her into a conversation, but she is only interested in the envelope that the man upstairs has given me. Often I contemplate pointing out to her the absurdity of this exchange. Why must she come to me when she could just as easily go to the man from Urada? I know it is entirely possible that she is unaware of his existence—in my husband's line of work, everything is cloaked in secrecy. No one knows the affairs of the person sitting next to him. You may be best friends with someone who shares your office space and not know how he passes his days, whom he talks to on the telephone. For this reason I have never mentioned to Hanna the man from Urada. But I also keep quiet because I recognize the delicacy of my position. I do not want to be demoted from my role as middleman; it is the only connection I have with my husband.

Friday mornings I drive to the Old City and purchase expensive liqueurs and gourmet teas in anticipation of Hanna's evening visit. I spend most of the day cleaning. In the afternoon I set the dining room table with interesting placeware that Jake has gathered from his various travels: a porcelain samovar from Uzbekistan, a gold serving spoon he bartered from a street trader in Zagreb. On a platter from the once beautiful Mostar I lay out a variety of cheeses, delicate finger sandwiches, chocolates I would never buy for myself. When Hanna arrives I open the door wide and invite her inside, hoping to entice her with the elaborate spread. I am certain that if she were to sit down with me, if we were to talk one woman to another, she could tell me things about my husband, things I need to know. I can feel her weakening, moving slowly toward me. On that first Friday, months ago, she wouldn't cross the threshold. The next time, she stepped just inside the doorway. On the third, she walked all the way into the foyer. Once, she even came far enough to glance into the empty stairwell where only moments before the man from Urada had stood in his bathrobe, gazing down at me. Still, Hanna has never accepted the food I offer. Sometimes she will talk with me about the weather or some item in the newspaper, but as soon as I mention my husband, she becomes all business. "Where is the envelope?" she says as kindly as possible. "I should be getting home."

Always I follow her out to her car, a purple T-bird with tinted windows and two oversized antennae, and ask for information about Jake. "Your husband's fine," is all she will say, tucking the envelope into a side pocket of the driver-side door. A couple of weeks ago, when Hanna gave her rote response—"Your husband's fine"—I said, "Maybe so. But I'm not."

She rolled down the window as she backed down the driveway. "I don't talk to him personally, but I'll pass on the word that he needs to get in touch with you."

It was a kind and human gesture amid this bureaucratic chaos, but it will be a difficult promise on which to deliver. I have read enough to know that information doesn't travel easily in that country. There are few street names in Urbistan. Someone can go there and just disappear.

I don't expect to hear from Jake any time in the near future. We are husband and wife, and he thinks this fact should suffice, should make up for any lack of communication. To him, our marital status serves as evidence of his love. What he doesn't understand is that it's not his love that is in question, merely his devotion. I try not to think about my husband's tastes. He admires the dowdy shapes and drab colors of the Urbistanian women's clothes—skirts and heels wherever they go, that awkward Eastern European style that is somehow

PROPAGANDA

sexy despite itself. In the early days of our relationship, when we were merely lovers and not in love, when I still found his interest in other women to be erotic rather than threatening, Jake confessed his obsession with the outlines of thighs beneath the heavy winter fabrics, the slope of a breast barely visible under a loose black cardigan. You can see the Urbistanian women dressed that way in the old propaganda videos, driving tractors and plowing fields.

"Many international experts agree that women in Urbistan enjoy an equality unparalleled elsewhere in the world," the narrator's voice says. The voice provides no concrete statistics. Everything is a generous guess presented belligerently as fact. "A large percentage of highly renowned industrial leaders agree that Urbistan is at the forefront of technology."

"Don't believe a word they say," Jake said the last time we watched one of the propaganda videos together. This was a few days before he left for Urbistan. That night he wore my favorite lipstick, Russian Red, which is not made by Russians of course but by MAC, a stylish Canadian cosmetics company. When we finished making love I turned on the light and stood in front of the vanity mirror. He had left his mark all over me, red smudges on my nipples, navel, and thighs.

THE SECOND TIME I accepted money for sex was not so long ago. I was bored. Christmas and Easter and Secretary's Day had passed with Jake in Urbistan. I was getting old.

I have a friend who writes articles for *Sports Illustrated*. He came to Knoxville to do a story about the Silver Bullets, the first professional women's baseball team since the barnstormers of the forties. This friend and I went to two practice games together. At the second game, he had a hot dog and I had vanilla ice cream in a little paper cup. After the game, in his red Rover sedan, he kissed me. His mouth tasted like spicy mustard. In his pocket he had sheets of miniature yellow legal pad paper which crinkled when he leaned over to kiss me. We had known each other since high school, and he felt casual with me. After the kiss he asked, "What would it take to get you in bed?"

"Twenty dollars."

It was a joke, of course, but when I woke up the next morning I found my moccasin on the pillow, and inside it he had stuffed a twenty-dollar bill. I know it wasn't right to play this game with him. The game is off-limits. It belongs to me and Jake. At least we didn't use the cowboys 'n' Indians sheets. Plain white instead. Cotton. Stolen from the Holiday Inn in Dumphries, Virginia, where Jake and I stayed one weekend while he was in training at the institute.

"Ankle," the caller's voice says. "Belly button. Breasts." He pauses for my reaction. I do not respond.

"Nipple," he whispers.

I think of Jake in the quiet dark of some small Urada apartment. Voices drift up from the street. The bed is narrow. The woman beside him is solemn. Their dark clothes lie heaped together in a large wicker basket. He touches her ankle, her belly button, her breast. With one finger he circles her nipple.

ON MOVING DAY a truck appears in the driveway, and two young men in blue uniforms arrive at my doorstep. The man from Urada keeps vigil behind the glass door. As I place the boxes beside the door to be carried out by the moving men, he sits at the top of his steps drinking something out of a small brown cup. I am wearing a long orange dress with no slip. The dress is only slightly transparent.

I have packed everything neatly into boxes—plates and cups and serving bowls, books and photo albums, Jake's shoes, the twenty-dollar bill that serves as evidence of my prostitution. There is a large box marked "Paraphernalia" that I have not bothered to close. The cardboard flaps gape, the evidence bares itself. I hope the moving men open it. If they dared give in to curiosity they would understand me in an instant.

"Housewife," they would tell their boss back at the office. "The most normal-looking ones are always the wildest."

The paraphernalia box contains straps and ropes and climbing devices, pinafores and collars, garish tubes of lipstick, Mary Janes, studded things and battery gadgets, and an assortment of leather goods, things designed to cause pain, desire, humiliation, intense levels of pleasure. But the movers do not care one bit. They are the picture of professionalism. They load large items first—the couch and the bed and the dining room table, the desk and the leopard-print chair. After that come the boxes, which they handle expertly. I sit on the steps of the apartment and when they are done I wait for them to come for me, the final item, to place me with care in the back of the truck among my husband's secret things. But they only say, "Is that all?"

"Yes."

"Please sign."

I sign.

"What about me?" I say, but they are already driving away.

I go inside to say good-bye to the man from Urada. For this occasion I have planned a passionate kiss, my lips pressed to his against the cool, slick barrier of glass, our fingertips aligned. We will say good-bye to one another the way they do in movies about love affairs. He will pass one last envelope under the door, addressed not to Jake but to me, a confession of his love. We will always remember this moment. But the man from Urada is no longer sitting in his stairwell. I can hear footsteps above me. He is going about his business. I press my face to the glass hoping to discover some scent of him, some faint odor of aftershave or food, but there is nothing. It is only at that moment that I realize what has happened: I have been removed from the conspiratorial loop.

SIX YEARS AGO, before he took the job and before we fell in love, Jake went to Urbistan with another woman, his first wife. In my mind I try to make peace with that place, but it is impossible. Since moving to Lillian Street I have neither seen nor heard from the man from Urada. Hanna's visits have stopped. I receive and pass on no information. All I have to go on now, all I have to remind me of the place my husband lives, are the books he bought for me—the works of Riljkin and Kajane, and a few articles printed in obscure journals. I also have two photographs, which I have placed between the covers of my red leather Bible—a gift from Grace years ago, when I planned to be a missionary. I did not choose that book out of religious conviction, but because it is the book I am least likely to open. I keep the photos in case Jake does not return to me, in case of death or disappearance.

In one, Jake and his ex-wife are sitting on a tousled bed in a room at an elaborate hotel. A plate of bread rests on the white sheets between them. Two bites have been taken. They lean toward one another, their hands touching behind the plate. Back when we were only sleeping together, not in love, when Jake and I could discuss past relationships with ease, he told me they had been the only guests in the hotel that night. The restaurant had to be opened just for them. When they entered the dining room they saw that all the tables were set perfectly, the napkins folded upright. A fine dust settled on the plates and glasses. During the night they heard the staff playing cards in a nearby room.

And this. Picture Jake, tall and gaunt and elegant, standing in the dim kitchen of a tiny apartment in the port town of Drarkes. He is leaning over the counter, holding a glass of water. Three chairs have been pulled up to a small table. In one chair sits his wife, with a small boy in her lap. On the far side of the table a woman: late-thirties, perhaps, lovely and smiling, with dark circles beneath her eyes. The third chair is empty. The teenage daughter stands beside it, a less tired version of her mother, staring into the camera with the unintentional, bored seduction of adolescence. She is wearing a silver bracelet and long misshapen skirt. It is a trick of the photo, the illusion of two-dimensional vision, that makes it seem as though her arm might be touching the front of Jake's shirt, her skirt brushing the tops of his shoes. There is an intimate disarray to the scene, a familiarity. On the day the photo was taken, Jake and his wife had been staying in the apartment for six days. They had only met the family a week ago, friends of a friend of a friend.

It is not the bedroom scene that disturbs me. There are bedrooms and lovers; I have been in such situations. There is food and drink and lovemaking. What undoes me is the image of Jake and his wife thrust into this family scene: the intimate chaos of day-to-day living, the harmony of physical discomfort, cramped spaces, the two of them presented as a unit, a permanent thing. When Jake thinks of the kindness of strangers in Drarkes, he will always think of her. To the family themselves, the mother and the boy and the voluptuous teenage daughter, Jake and his wife will always appear together in the replay of memory, in conversations about the couple from America. I do not exist.

"ANKLE," THE MAN said last night.

I was grateful for his voice, its familiarity in this new place, the sound reaching toward me from the darkness, inside the blue walls of the house on Lillian Street.

"Belly button . . . breasts . . . nipples." His voice in the quiet confusion of my half-sleep was like water rising beneath the white sheets, a welcome warmth.

"How did you get this number?"

"Vagina," he whispered.

"Jake?" I said. It did not matter to me who it was. I just wanted him to pretend.

"Vagina," he repeated.

I was silent.

"What kind of woman are you?" the caller said. "Did you hear what I just said?"

He hung up. I went back to sleep. I dreamt of Jake lying in a giant basket. A woman with long black hair pulled the ropes that lifted the basket over the city walls. Jake watched and listened, took notes in his little yellow pad. "Good-bye," he said at last to the handsome basket woman, kissing her on the mouth. Jake hid himself away in another city, where he passed on vital information. Some blood was shed. Some lives were lost. "All in the line of duty," he said, saluting me from across the miles, the mountains, the slumbering Adriatic.

EVERY NOW AND then I drive by the house on Amelia Street. A woman with a small red Toyota much like mine has moved into the downstairs apartment. Once I saw her walking up to the door with a bag of groceries, then turning the key in the lock.

Sometimes, late at night, I go there and watch the informant. Not long ago, I saw him standing beside a purple lamp, staring out the second floor window. If he noticed me sitting in my car across the street, headlights off, window down, he did not acknowledge me. I considered going to him, persuading him that neither of us was needed anymore, that it was time to abandon Jake, who kept us waiting, day after day, month after month, while his own thoughts turned so rarely to us. I had made the decision, rehearsed my speech, and was walking up the sidewalk to the house when I saw a second figure move into the lamplight. Her hair fell past her shoulders. She was not particularly shapely or beautiful. She was not wearing any clothes. As she stood before him, he pressed one hand to her breast and I realized she was the woman who had rented my apartment. The scene remained this way for some time. All that moved was her mouth. She was saying something to him. He seemed to be listening. At last they moved away from the window. I kept watching anyway, for some sign of him. A woman's voice carried to me through the darkness—it was nothing more than a moan, a letting go of air. In a little while his figure passed again through the frame of the window, slowly. His shoulders were bent. He was naked. He stretched and turned off the lamp. In the moment before the light disappeared I could see the soft tangle of hair in his armpit, and I imagined that her scent lingered there; in the morning he would wake, lift his arms to stretch, and be startled by the womanish smell.

I don't know how long I had been standing there on the sidewalk, looking up at the window, when the front door of my old apartment opened and the woman came out of it. "What are you doing?" she said.

"I used to live here."

"Well, I live here now."

Face to face, it struck me that this woman looked much like me: the light brown hair, the pale skin, the downward curve of the mouth. She wore gray sweatpants and a shapeless button-down. In one hand she held a piece of fruit, and in the other, some sort of garment that dripped water onto the porch. "You best be going." That was all.

I took the long way home—down Rule, right on Sutherland and over the railroad tracks, past Brunson Light and Lamp, where dozens of chandeliers sparkled behind the plateglass windows. I drove past the pawnshop with the drag queen mannequin sitting spread-eagle in the window. She wore a pink satin nightgown, thick rouge on her high, shining cheekbones, a Jackie O hat to cover her baldness. It was two in the morning. Behind the brick walls of JFG Coffee Company the workers were grinding hundreds of pounds of coffee; the air reeked of it, nutty and rich and slightly burnt.

As I rounded the curve past the cemetery and into my driveway, I thought of the man from Urada, his hand on the woman's breast. That he could place his hands on another woman—or worse, lie awake at night thinking of her, dreaming of the time and place they would meet—was unimaginable. Inside the empty house I washed my hair, brushed my teeth, and crawled beneath the covers, which still smelled of the house on Amelia Street. Every time I closed my eyes, they opened again of their own volition. Through the night I found myself staring at a wedding photo on the bedside table. In the photo I am wearing a blue satin dress. Jake rests an extraordinarily white hand on my bare shoulder. One finger is tucked beneath the strap of my dress. With the other hand he plunges a large silver knife into the snowy wedding cake.

All night I breathed and waited. Not once did the telephone ring.

Curvature

*C*elia grew up unable to dance because of the scoliosis, because of the Milwaukee brace she wore twenty-three hours a day
beginning in second grade. So she taught her fingers to dance. The
living room was her ballroom. The piano by the fireplace obeyed.
Celia could play "The Entertainer" with both hands. She'd find middle C and go from there. She knew a whole book of church hymns
by heart: "Have Thine Own Way Lord" and "When the Saints Go
Marchin' In."

Seventh grade. Boys don't know what to say to a girl who wears a
back brace. To seventh grade boys a girl is simply the sum of her
parts: metal from neck to tailbone, hard plastic on the rib cage, white
pads against her chin that hold her head high and still.

I remember her, age twelve through seventeen, in exactly this
way: black eyes squinting over a needle, head bent, all the world
unknown to her. The needle's tiny point pierces in and out, in and

out. Her lips move but make no sound as she counts the stitches, one, two, three. Or her hands fly in little circles, a wad of yarn unrolling on the floor as two long needles click-click-click, and miraculously a blanket or baby booties take shape between her hands. The walls of our parents' house are covered with unframed squares of cloth depicting peaceful, happy scenes, stitch by perfect stitch, thread by meticulous thread.

"Here, let me show you," Celia used to say. "It's just a simple chain stitch." But my hands couldn't learn, my fingers wouldn't work.

Now Celia is married to a man named Robert who takes her to country-western bars. She knows every step of the cotton-eyed Joe. Home for Christmas, on the front lawn of our parents' house with the grass still green in Mobile's winter heat, she says to me, "It's easy. Put your feet like this, see, and count." Celia's little daughter, Roberta, stands on the sidewalk watching. *One two three*, she claps. *Four five six*. But my feet are no better than my fingers, and to this day I can't match numbers to movements, can't tap out a tune on the piano or do the tush push to a cadence of one, two, three.

Now Celia has a metal rod up her spine to make it straight, they sliced her open and put it there. Her back will never bend. The scar is shaped like three quarters of a moon turning on a raw celestial axis. For several days after the surgery she lay on her stomach, a bright red C of blood seeping through the gauze. On Celia's wedding day, her dress scooped low to show the scar that made her straight. Six days before the wedding I entered her bedroom while she was sleeping, lowered the sheet, ran my finger along the scar. It felt like silk, not skin, slick to the touch and minutely wrinkled. I remembered how, years before, my mother had lifted the soiled white gauze and carefully redressed the wound as I watched from the doorway, envying them both that one last gesture of intimacy in a long history of intimacies.

"If you had several children and one of them was stricken with leprosy, would you leave the healthy children to accompany the sick one to the leper's colony?" I had asked.

Startled, my mother turned to me. "I didn't realize you were there."

"Would you?"

She did not even pause to consider. "Of course," she said, moving her hands with the utmost tenderness across my sister's bruised back.

Mathematics

and

Acrobatics

$\mathscr{S}$ometimes the stripe is metallic silver, sometimes it is gray-ish blue, but other than that single flash of color there is no variation. The back of the bus wavers, shimmying side to side. By instinct I brake slightly, putting distance between us. Suddenly the bus spins around, full tilt, the stripe flashing in the snowy light, and then the front end of it is facing me. I catch a glimpse of the driver's face just before the whole thing slides off the road and over the embankment. He looks surprised more than anything, as if he doesn't know what to do. Looking into his face I think, "So this is it. This is how it ends: a cold day on Atlanta's Perimeter." It is that quick, and then it is over.

My daughter, strapped into the backseat, saw the bus turn over, somersault she called it. She counted four somersaults before the stunned vehicle came to rest on its side. In the moments after the bus went down I had my attention on the road, swerving around the patch of snow that was later named as one in a number of culprits.

Other factors included speed and a blood alcohol level just one tenth this side of legal. It was the middle of January, the third snow of an unseasonably cold winter.

While she was counting the somersaults, my daughter was also counting the flyers. That's what she called them: "I saw eight flyers coming from eight windows." She has a head for math, that one, although the number later reported in the papers was ten.

"Flyers?" I asked.

"People flying out the windows," she said excitedly. "One of them was wearing a red dress. I could see her underwear! It was white. I bet she was surprised?" She was looking at me for confirmation, wanting to know if the woman in the red dress had indeed been surprised as she hurtled through the chilled air toward her death. My daughter sees the world in terms of mathematics and acrobatics. For her, it may as well have been one big circus.

In a matter of seconds—four, maybe five—I glimpsed in my rear-view mirror the spot of road where the bus had been. It looked perfectly normal, that empty length of road, save for two wide skid marks and the motorists who pulled onto the shoulder, one after the other. I could see them getting out of their cars, not even bothering to shut the doors behind them, running down the embankment to help. Later, I would come up with many reasons to forgive myself for not being among them: namely, that there are things you don't want a seven-year-old child to see—dead bodies strewn across the snow, severed limbs, victims screaming from beneath the wreckage.

A couple of minutes later we pulled into Dairy Queen. I got out of the car, opened my daughter's door, unbuckled her seatbelt, and held her. I was waiting for her to cry, waiting for the terror to kick in, the full impact of what she had just seen—blood, destruction, large-scale sudden death. There were no tears, though, nothing.

"Do you think those people are dead?" she asked. I looked at her. Her eyes were so round and demanding, her father's deep brown eyes. She has his eyebrows too—bushy, unkempt, already crossing the bridge over her nose. I imagined the eyebrows would be a curse when she got older, just one more thing she'd have to keep under control, the object of continual anxious plucking. She seemed at that moment like someone else's child, a child I hardly knew. "Those flyers," she said. "I bet they all died."

I tried to hold her a bit longer, but she squirmed out of my arms. "What are we doing here?" she asked. I took her inside for a chocolate sundae to get her mind off things. "It's okay, baby," I said, wiping my eyes, trying to be steadfast like the mothers in movies. The mothers in movies turn away just before the tears begin to flow. Or they hug you, their pained faces to the camera, their tears falling, unknown, down your back. The mothers in movies exhibit great strength and gentle fortitude for the sake of their children.

Roberta, unmoved, looked up at me. Chocolate dripped down her chin. "What's okay?" she said.

YOU WAIT FOR the trauma, the aftershock. You take them to therapy. You are certain they're holding it in. You want to believe that you have a normal child, full of conflicting emotions, a child who can be scarred by such an event if she is not paid the proper attention. But this is what the therapist told me: "Your daughter feels nothing. She is unhealthily detached."

I refused to accept this. I told the therapist that he was wrong, that my child was simply slow to respond. "My child," I called her; sometimes, I confess, I find it difficult to use her name. It is her father's name. He chose it because I was at a loss. He suggested naming her Celia, after me, but I felt uncomfortable with the idea of having another person in the house who shared my name. So Robert took his own name and added a single letter, and in the weeks after she was born it began to make sense: she looked just like him, nose and eyes and mouth, ears and hair, everything. It was a wonder to me that she had come from my body. I saw nothing of myself in her. Nursing her, rubbing her soft back, cradling the whole of her infant body in my hands, I would look down at that round, sweet-smelling head covered with brown hair and think, "Who is this child?" I gave all of the physical affection a mother is supposed to give, all of the attention necessary to create a loving and well-adjusted individual, but I often wonder if she could sense in me, even then, a missing thing: some lack of warmth or feeling, some failure to connect.

"Roberta is still processing the event," I said to the therapist, forcing her name off my tongue, hoping he wouldn't see through me. "Give her time."

I tried to plan the proper responses for the inevitable questions: "What happens when you die? Did those people go to heaven? What if you die, mommy? What if daddy dies?" The questions never came. Instead, my daughter said things like, "If that bus did not fall off the road we would have hit it, you and me. Splat." She smacked her hands together for emphasis, rolled her head back like a dead person, stuck her tongue out of her mouth in what might have been a comical pose, were it not for the seriousness of the subject matter. "I'm glad the bus fell off the road," she said. "Aren't you?"

"That's a terrible thing to say."

But Roberta was right, of course. Had it not gone over, my daughter and I would have collided with the bus. There is no doubt we both would have been killed. Perhaps it would have been just the two of us, rather than the eleven who died that day en route to Biloxi, Mississippi, most of them senior citizens. Perhaps a collision with a small vehicle such as ours would have interrupted the bus's momentum, played havoc with the forces of velocity and speed, halted its quadruple roll down the frozen embankment. Mathematically speaking, it would have been better for the two of us to die, rather than the eleven.

The bus driver, one and a half beers to the wind at ten o'clock in the morning, was unharmed, just a single long gash above his right eyebrow. That night, in the news footage that ran over and over again on the local stations, he could be seen wandering amid the wreckage, dazed, while the dead and injured bled great quantities of blood into the snow. It's amazing what they'll show, the pictures they'll give you. More gruesome photographs appeared in the *Atlanta Journal Constitution* the following day, along with details. Ruth Nelson, whose leg was located a quarter-mile from her body, survived, saved by a heart condition that caused her blood to clot. Her husband died from internal injuries. A twenty-nine-year-old teacher went into a coma out of which she was not expected to awake. They'll tell you anything in the papers, as if you have a right to know, as if the whole world is the victim's next of kin.

The day after the accident Robert and I read the morning paper together, trading sections as we completed them, exchanging bits of information: the bus driver was fifty-two; the passengers had before them a day of minor gambling; the fatalities included eight women and three men; one woman remained alive for three hours, pinned under the bus, holding the hand of one of the rescue workers.

"I have to admit I'm surprised," Robert said, staring down into his cereal bowl.

"About what?"

"I'm surprised you didn't pull over."

"Plenty of people stopped to help. I wasn't needed."

"Still," he said.

"You weren't there."

The TV was on in the next room. Roberta was watching some cartoon about a gang of sarcastic, sloppily dressed children who played nasty pranks on the adults in their lives. Their dialogue was spiced with double entendre, sexual innuendo.

"Should she be watching that stuff?" Robert said.

"I don't think she gets it. If she doesn't get it, it probably can't corrupt her."

I shoved the newspaper into the trash can. That evening I found Roberta lying on the living room floor, the paper spread out in front of her. She had retrieved it from the garbage, wiped away the coffee grinds and citrus rinds, and cut out the photos of the accident. She had already pasted the big, front-page photo into her scrapbook. The picture, taken from the road above the wreckage, showed the bus lying on its side, looking off balance but unharmed save for a few shattered windows, surrounded by bodies.

"Where did you get that?" I asked, gathering the crumpled pages from the floor. She looked up at me and rolled her eyes, as if I were the crazy one. I noticed that her thick black bangs needed to be cut; when she blinked, her eyelashes caught against them. Roberta hated for me to help her dress and she wouldn't let me get near her with a pair of scissors, and as a result, she often looked like a child with overworked parents, a girl whose mother didn't notice when she began to fall apart. "Why do you want to do this?" I asked, staring down at her scrapbook. She was an organized child, prone to categorization, labels, the morbid gathering of facts. She had already titled the page in black crayon with her clear hand, her impeccable spelling: *The Crash.*

A FUND WAS established in honor of the victims. The bus driver's name was splashed across the papers, along with a detailed account of his driving record. Witnesses came forward with harrowing details. Heroes were named: the emergency rescue team that worked for four hours to extract the survivors from the wreckage, the girl in the red sports utility vehicle, on her way to a camping trip, who scrambled down the embankment with blankets and sleeping bags in tow to shield the bodies of the dead from the gaze of passersby. The girl's sound bite was repeated dozens of times on the local twenty-four-hour news station: "Everybody deserves a little dignity. If it was my mom out there, I'd want somebody to do the same." Having covered the fatalities, she went back to her vehicle and got water for the survivors. "I didn't really know what to do. I just wanted to help however I could until the ambulances arrived."

In the news clip, shot on-site about an hour after the accident, the heroine is wearing a green sweatshirt, jeans, and a yellow scarf. She is beautiful, teary-eyed but tough, the kind of hero the public can really latch on to. Hillary Keyman is a third-year student at Emory, a biology major who'd been doing work-study in the animal research department of the medical school before the crash that catapulted her to a position of local celebrity. Her job was to inject mice with drugs that would increase their brain size. She then put the enlarged mice through mazes to test their mental fortitude. Hillary appeared on a local television show called *Acts of Kindness*. The host of the show asked her about others who had stopped to help. She related several heartwarming stories. Then she said, "I remember this one car, this blue Toyota. It was directly behind the bus. The woman was going too fast. Right before the bus went over, she tried to pass it."

"You're kidding," the host said, indignant. The audience got involved. The camera shot a close-up of a man with hair plugs dotted across his forehead like ink spots. The man stood up and said, "We got two kind of people in this world, people like you and then people like that woman in the blue car."

YES, I HAD TRIED to pass. I remembered that. But there wasn't room, a car had sped up behind in the next lane just as I was trying to maneuver around the bus. I had dropped back. Surely there was no relationship between the accident and my failed pass. Hillary Keyman repeated the story about the blue Toyota to a print journalist as well, who speculated that I had been at the root of the accident, that I was just as guilty as the snowdrift and the bus driver.

"You know none of it is true, don't you?" I asked Robert one night in bed.

"I know, baby," he said. To his credit, he was trying to be on my side. But when you've been married to a man for twelve years, you know what he's really thinking, even if he won't tell you.

In the weeks following the accident, I dreamt often of mice with oversize heads tunneling through bloody mazes, or chewing through

84

the steering cables of huge tour buses. I dreamt of the heroine in her green sweatshirt, engaged in everyday activities such as picking Roberta up from school, or balancing my checkbook, or making love to Robert. The dreams were so real that when I awoke I was not only relieved, but surprised, to find Robert in bed beside me, snoring softly. Awake, I found myself thinking, *She would probably make a wonderful mother. She would probably do everything right.*

"EVERYTHING OKAY?" Robert asked Roberta one night. He was sitting on the edge of her bed, having tucked the blanket high up around her chin. I watched from the hallway. A night-light in the shape of a polar bear glowed dimly in a corner of her room. I noticed that Robert's neck needed shaving. He looked unkempt and lovely, his body bent forward in the low light, every ounce of his attention invested at that moment in his daughter. I wonder, sometimes, how he does it: that complete surrender to another human being, that sure and selfless devotion to our child. Either one of us would die for her, without question. But I have always harbored the uncomfortable feeling that Robert's love goes beyond mine, somehow, that he believes without doubt that he was meant to be not only a father, but the father of this very girl—Roberta in her blue pajamas, with her bushy eyebrows and low, long-winded laugh.

I, on the other hand, do not feel suited to motherhood. *A child,* I thought, when the doctor gave me the news. It seemed like a ferocious undertaking, a lifelong project I wasn't really up to. Robert was thrilled; I assumed I would eventually share his excitement. When I mentioned my unease, my mother said, "Wait until it's your own! Something in you just clicks, and it feels, well, right."

So I waited for the click. I imagined I would both hear it and feel it, like an engine turning over, something certain and identifiable. But it didn't happen: not three months into the pregnancy, not six, not on the day she was born. "Post-partum depression," my friends told me. I was too ashamed to admit, months later, that the depression had never gone away. Watching Roberta in her crib, I found her sweet, vulnerable, perfect even; but I never thought, "This is the best thing I've ever done, my greatest achievement to date." I thought of my own mother, so attentive to me through my childhood. I wondered if it was my frailty that had made her love me so: my curved back, my undersized lungs, the doctors always telling her that I was lucky to be alive. If only Roberta could be weaker, less sure of herself, perhaps I could muster the proper emotions.

"If there's anything you want to talk about," Robert said, his face so close to hers that their noses touched.

"You mean the bus," our daughter said.

"Anything."

I was listening to him, loving him still after twelve years of marriage. But lately, over breakfast, Robert and I had little to talk about except the drapery store we own and manage or some item in the newspaper. Our child seemed to be a blank wall, devoid of emotion, forever involved in the act of counting. She counted the socks in her drawer, the number of tiles on the bathroom floor, the exact number of minutes and seconds it took for a moth to die once she trapped it under a jar.

The night-light flickered out; it was just their voices then. "Mommy didn't stop."

"What?"

"After the bus fell off the road, all these cars stopped to help, but Mommy kept driving. Why didn't she stop?"

"She didn't want you to see things that would frighten you."

"I'm old enough."

I stepped back, suddenly afraid that she might see me standing there in the dim light of the hallway.

"Why did you want to stop?" Robert asked.

There was a pause. She cleared her throat. That was what Roberta did when she was hedging, deciding whether or not to tell. "I

86

counted eight flyers," she whispered. "On the news they said there were ten that went out the window, but I only counted eight. I wanted to see what they looked like after they hit the ground. This woman in the red dress? I saw her picture in the paper. Part of her leg was missing."

She waited for Robert to say something. He was silent. I knew he was trying to find the right words.

"Did you hear me?" she demanded, the pitch of her voice rising. "I said part of her leg came *off.*"

"That's enough."

"What." Roberta meant it not as a question, but a challenge. "What!" she repeated more loudly.

"I said that's enough." For the first time I could remember, he was stumped.

"She's right," he said that night, as we were lying in bed, our thighs touching beneath the sheets. I wanted to make love. I had removed my bathrobe in the dark, slipped into bed, and waited for Robert to crawl in beside me. I thought it would excite him, to find me naked like that, and waiting, my skin still warm from the bath. Now I rolled onto my side and laid a leg on top of him, over his stomach.

"Who's right?" I said softly, pressing my mouth to his ear.

"You should have stopped."

I rolled onto my back, surprised and a little angry. "She's seven years old. I made the only call that seemed appropriate at the time. A wreck of that magnitude is the kind of thing that could haunt a kid forever—all the blood, all those people dying."

"You stopped at Dairy Queen, for God's sake. You bought Roberta an ice cream sundae, like it's just an ordinary day."

"You think you would have done differently?"

"Yes."

"You can't know unless you're there."

"Sometimes you just do what's right," he said then, in the kind of tone you might take with a child, not with an equal. "It's that simple."

YOU HEAR ABOUT people going over the edge. You never imagine it might happen to you. I remember it now as a feeling of vertigo, a gradual slipping.

I am sitting at the kitchen table, the white pages spread out in front of me, open to K. *Katz, Kent, Kesler.* I cannot believe it's there in black and white for anyone to see. *Keyman, Hillary.* Not just an initial, but her full name.

The white pages remain open on the kitchen table for hours. I have taken a few days off from the store. I am the only one home. I complete various household tasks—laundry, dishes, the transfer of photos into albums—coming back every few minutes to the table and staring down at the phone book. I have memorized her phone number. At 2:00 in the afternoon I call her. She is home. I tell her only my first name. "I was there," I say. "At the accident. I've seen you in the papers. I'd like to talk."

There is a pause, perhaps a moment of deliberation during which Hillary Keyman decides whether or not to be gracious. Maybe she's wondering how long this thing is going to last, wanting her life back the way it was before the accident.

"Okay," she says finally. "I've got some errands in Little Five Points tomorrow. How about the Russian Pastry Shop?"

"Perfect," I say, feeling grateful and relieved, thinking that I can make her understand.

AT THE COUNTER I order two coffees, a chocolate croissant, and an apple strudel, then take the only available table, a two-top barely big enough for one. The Russian Pastry Shop is packed with college students, most of them ten to fifteen years younger than I, and staffed by beautiful girls in tight black pants with dark circles under their eyes. Sitting here, waiting, I feel my age in a way I seldom do. I

MATHEMATICS AND ACROBATICS

want to go home and change into some youthful disguise, some other outfit that would not announce so loudly that I am a wife and mother, a woman who no longer lives inside of things, who, in fact, isn't even sure what the inside of things looks like any more. At the next table a dark-haired guy in his mid-twenties sits reading. He is good-looking and a little sloppy, the kind of guy I might have gone for a long time ago, before Robert passed me the ring over a bottle of wine he couldn't afford at a small, dark restaurant in Buckhead. As the ring lay beside my silverware, looking no more or less shiny than the spoon and fork, I said, "That was sweet of you, Robert," unable to think of anything more profound.

After a couple of minutes the young man glances up from his book and catches me staring, but instead of returning my gaze, he looks back to his book, indifferent. I wonder if he can discern in my posture, in the clean dullness of my hair, in the utilitarian way I handle the croissant like a woman who eats for sustenance rather than for the sensual joy of it–that I am the co-owner of a small drapery business, that I haven't been dancing in years. I want to tell him that I don't remember exactly when I stopped looking in the mirror before I left the house, or when I began purchasing comfortable underwear and going to bed at a reasonable hour, sober even on weekends.

For half an hour I wait, skimming *Creative Loafing*, pretending to be interested in various articles attacking the mayor, the government, the police. I scan *The Back Page*, where Atlantans with a romantic weakness send out desperate pleas to people they believe they were meant to be with—people who escaped them after a brief, accidental encounter in a public place. *You: blue shoes, bag of plums. Me: blonde hair, reading the paper. We exchanged smiles in the gift shop of Fernbank Museum, 11/24. You purchased a dinosaur puzzle. Would like to exchange more. Please call Dave at–*. The bad ink blurs, the messages rub off on my hands. I imagine Dave sitting by the phone, mentally abusing himself for not having gotten her number. You

89

know how these things work. Blue Shoes will never call. Dave will place the ad two or three more times. He'll go to Fernbank Museum for several weeks running, at the same time he saw her there. Desperate, he'll look for her face in the crowd. After a few weeks he'll give up, but he will always remember her, thinking he made a grave error, thinking he could have had the life he always wanted, if only he'd asked her name. Every other woman Dave meets will have to compete with blue shoes, bag of plums.

After half an hour, I eat the apple strudel I ordered for Hillary Keyman, certain that she has stood me up. I'm wiping the crumbs off the table when she walks in, wearing a fitted black jacket and no makeup, radiating the kind of energetic beauty that family men often rediscover, like a long-forgotten prize, sometime after their fortieth birthday. Hillary Keyman's blonde hair tumbles over her shoulders in an alluring way. I consider ducking out of the shop before she can identify me, slipping into my car and returning to my private world of guilt and anonymity. But she is already coming toward me, having spotted my red sweater I suppose, the one with the snowflake collar, the one I told her I'd be wearing.

The tables are packed so tightly that the dark-haired guy has to scoot his chair over a couple of inches so Hillary can get in hers. "Sorry," she says to him, stepping on the end of his scarf where it trails the floor.

"That's quite all right," he says, looking up at her.

"Thanks for coming," I say.

"Sorry I'm late." She fidgets with her watchband and looks around the room, as if she might find someone more interesting in the crowd. "You were there?" she says. "I'm sorry; you don't look familiar." She sips her coffee, then pushes it away. "Has it been very difficult for you? It has for me, knowing that some of them were alive right after it happened. I think the worst thing is knowing I may have been the last face someone saw before they died. You must know what I mean."

The dark-haired guy keeps looking up from his book and staring at her, the way you look at someone when you're trying to decide whether or not you've met somewhere before. I want him to go away, I don't want him to hear this. I rehearsed in the car all the way over—my confession and the accompanying explanation, my plea for understanding.

"I'm sure you know what I mean," she repeats. Her voice is matter-of-fact. "I was just thinking that if it was my own mother out there, I'd want someone to be calm for her. I'd want her last moments to be peaceful."

I came seeking some kind of absolution. When I looked her up in the phone book yesterday, I was certain that if I could just tell her my side, she would understand. I wanted her to know that the bus had lost control several seconds after I tried to pass, that there was really no correlation. I fantasized about her coming home with me for dinner and taking Roberta aside, saying, "Your mother was only trying to protect you." She would tell Robert that he shouldn't blame me, that my attempt to pass the bus had nothing to do with the accident. Surely if he heard it from her he would concede and things could go back to normal, he would start trusting me again.

Hillary's voice is matter-of-fact. "I was just thinking that if it was my own mother out there, I'd want someone to be calm for her. I'd want her last moments to be peaceful."

"Of course. It was terrible to see their faces," I say, lying with an ease that astounds me. "A man died in my arms. That's why I came here. I needed to share it with you. He was lying there, and I was holding him, and his breaths were very shallow but I believed if I could just stay with him until the paramedics arrived he would live."

Hillary reaches over and holds my hands. "You did everything you could. You couldn't have been expected to do more."

We stay for a while longer, reminiscing, trading stories. She thinks she remembers seeing me there; yes, my face is very familiar. The details come easily to me, as easily as memory. The man who died in my arms was wearing a navy sport coat, I say. Though quite old, he had not begun to go bald. He spoke incoherently about his parents' immigration from Eastern Europe. He remembered a lamppost in Athens, Georgia, beside which he often sat as a child, waiting for his mother to close the family-owned print shop and bring him a bar of chocolate.

The young man at the table next to us abandons his book, eaves-dropping without subtlety. When Hillary gets up to leave, there is panic on his face. I imagine the message he might post on the back page of *Creative Loafing: You: blonde hair, black jacket. You sat beside me at the Russian Pastry Shop. Wish I'd introduced myself. Please call.*

DRIVING HOME, I think about Robert, who will be sipping Scotch whiskey on the back patio when I arrive, playing checkers or Go Fish with Roberta. I move slowly through the afternoon haze, watching for random patches of ice, cars with missing taillights, eighteen-wheelers shattering the speed limit as they barrel toward certain disaster. As I drive, one foot on the accelerator and the other poised, anxious, above the brake, I reinvent the story for Robert. I will tell him that I met Hillary at Lenox Mall, that she is not as pretty in real life as she was on TV. I'll tell him she wears too much makeup and laughs too loudly. I'll say that she showed up with a University of Georgia student, her boyfriend, a senior with finicky hair. The more details, the better. The boyfriend wore a purple scarf. He talked on about some trip he'd made to Nairobi last summer, just before the bombings. I told her the truth. To Hillary's credit, she sympathized with me when she heard my story. She agreed that the accident was not my fault, and not something a seven-year-old should see. She said she had a nephew who was nine. If her nephew had been in the car, she too would have kept on driving. I try to pinpoint any holes in my story. I want it to be perfect.

A red Nissan begins to quake in front of me. For a moment I think it might lose a tire, spin into the median, land upside down in the frozen grass. I hope for that, my moment of redemption, my chance to prove myself. I have fantasized about it countless times since the accident: an entire family clinging to life by a thread, and me their only hope, giving mouth-to-mouth and pulling them carefully from the wreckage. It would be even better yet if the car were burning and I were gravely injured in the effort, thus reinstating my honor and saving my marriage. But the driver regains control, and disaster is averted. The Nissan rolls on in front of me, steady and safe.

The World's

Greatest

Pants

*a*bout the time she entered ninth grade, Darlene acquired a steadfastness my parents found insulting. They labeled her defiant, but in my eyes she was brave. During her sophomore year of high school, I came upon Darlene and my mother in the kitchen, their faces not two inches apart, Darlene shouting, "If I were old enough to vote I'd cast my ballot for Jimmy Carter, just to cancel you out." She might as well have confessed to a murder.

Every moment between the two of them was a confrontation. I think our mother could not comprehend a daughter who refused to be intimidated, a daughter who refused to wear makeup. Darlene was kicked out of Girls in Action, the Baptist version of the Girl Scouts, for complaining that the Royal Ambassadors got to do "all the fun shit." She ran track at school and didn't shave her legs. When she skipped senior prom to go see *Platoon* with one of her track-mates, my mother expressed aloud for the first time her concern that

Darlene might be funny. "I'm beginning to think you might be funny," were her exact words.

"Funny as in ha-ha?" Darlene said, propping her feet on the kitchen table.

"There's nothing ha-ha about being funny," our father interjected from the living room. He was watching the Weather Channel. A hurricane was chugging toward the Gulf Coast like a sluggish loco- motive, and he was excited.

Twenty minutes later I found Darlene in the back yard, sitting under the big oak tree with Baby, who was six years old that year. They were playing tic-tac-toe in the dirt, using acorns for playing pieces.

"Are you half-acorns or whole acorns?" I asked Darlene.

"Half." She didn't look up, but I could hear in her voice that she was crying. Her shoulders shook slightly and she kept her face turned toward the ground. I sat down beside her and said the only thing I could think of—"I play winner."

"What's wrong?" Baby said. She started to cry too. Then Celia came outside. That was the year she got two hours a day out of her brace, and she looked relaxed and elegant, so slender I envied her. She sat down in our circle. By that point I was crying.

"What's wrong with everybody?" Celia asked.

"Mom called Darlene funny," I said.

Our mother came outside with the camera. "Smile," she said. "I want to get a picture of all my girls together."

Darlene left home a few months later. She staged a departure so bold and unexpected that anything the rest of us would later do seemed insignificant in comparison. She showed up one evening in January with a small girl in red vinyl pants so shiny they looked as if they'd been waxed at the car wash. The girl drove an old blue El Camino and wore eyeglasses with big black frames. She stood the way girls stand in movies when they're about to do something rash, her hands in her hip pockets, looking bored, explosive, and sex-starved all at once. When we went out to greet them in the driveway, the girl slid her arm protectively around Darlene's waist.

"This is Beth," Darlene said, looking at Celia instead of my mother. "We've got a place in Bandera."

"Cool," Celia said.

My mother, at a loss, turned to me. "Where's Bandera?" she asked.

"Texas, maybe?"

Beth nodded and offered proudly, "It's the dude ranch capital of the world. My parents have some land."

"How many acres?" my mother asked, temporarily regaining her composure. Up until that moment, I think she held out some hope that Darlene would someday be a bride.

"Fifty," Beth said. I could almost hear my mother's mental calculator ticking off the land value.

Daddy had been standing by the back door, watching. "If you stay at home we could pay for you to go to the university," he said. Money was tight, but he was serious.

"Thanks," Darlene said, "but we've already decided."

"You don't even have to live with us," Daddy said. "Just stay in Mobile and we'll work everything out. We'll find you an apartment." Beth caught my eye and winked, like we were in on this together. I was embarrassed to have her witness my father's awkward desperation.

Beth helped Darlene load some clothes into the El Camino, while our parents stood by, silent. Baby wanted to know if she could come too. Celia and I promised to visit, and Daddy said quietly that we would do no such thing. When they were ready to go, my mother wrapped her arms around Darlene and held on so tight I thought we'd have to pry her fingers loose. "Mom," Darlene said. "It's just Texas."

When Beth reached out to shake my mother's hand, Mom folded her arms across her chest and backed away. "Just remember she's been my daughter for eighteen years," she said. "You can't change that."

Daddy stood under the carport, looking shocked and powerless, his arms hanging at his sides. "When are you coming back?"

"As soon as you invite us," Darlene said.

Later, Mom called Celia and me to the dining room table. "What I want for all of my girls is a comfortable situation, happiness, and a moral life," she said. "It is possible to have all three."

That night in bed I thought of Darlene and Beth in the shabby El Camino, driving through Texas, which must be as dark as it is big. I was filled up with pride for Darlene, who was old enough and strong enough to leave us. I thought of my sister with her hand on Beth's thigh, how those red vinyl pants would be warm beneath her fingers. I closed my eyes and remembered the world's greatest pants, and I fell asleep dreaming of that deep and miraculous shine.

Disneyland

*h*e takes six steps down the hallway to the living room, where he slaps the chandelier and it does its glassy rattle-tattle. On his shoulders I'm tall as the sun, slippety-slap his head's a drum. My mother arrives. He sets me down. Celia walks in, head high, back straight, the metal buckles of her back brace clinking as she goes. Darlene lies across the sofa, struggling with a Rubik's Cube.

We've all been gathered here today, he begins. It sounds like a joke but my mother isn't laughing, the stuffing's coming out of the gold chair in the corner, the ferns in the planter box are dying. *Lordie,* he says. *Uh-huh.* He's a white man from Mississippi who sounds like a Ray Charles song.

One room over, Baby's in her crib. Mother has painted the room with clouds and sheep. She even built a white picket fence that stands knee-high around the room. *Beautimus, beautiful, angel mine,* Daddy says whenever he sees the baby. Still, he never holds her, never puts her on his shoulders, which leads me to believe that I am the best-loved girl.

Gotta go, he says, sing-song, but it's nothing from the radio. I know right off he means it. *It's not your mother's fault, we don't get along, I'll be back to visit.* Three steps from the gold chair to the door, eight from door to truck, where his shirts hang neatly on a rod. Everything's been planned. He backs slowly down the driveway, waving with a smile on his face like he's going to Disneyland.

Intermittent

Waves of

Unusual Size

and Force

*F*rederick hit the summer he was gone. Three days after the hurricane, he came back to find the giant oak in the front yard stripped of all but four branches. Our house stood at the end of Epson Downs Street, and the debris from the tree blocked cars from passing through the neighborhood. That's the way he tells it. The way I remember it, five branches remained, not four, and the street was messy, but not entirely blocked. Dad's been known to exaggerate.

I was in the backyard selling pool water when I heard his truck pull into the driveway. The truck door rattled shut and he came through the tall wooden fence. I was surprised to see that he looked almost exactly the same; he'd been gone nearly two months by then. We'd learned to live without him.

Sammy Sousa, a lanky second-grader who belonged to the Catholic family four houses down, was standing on the top step of our

Doughboy pool. His sister Elaine waited on the lawn with two milk jugs he'd already filled with dirty pool water. She was only ten but she jutted her hip out the way her mother did and looked at Dad like he'd done something wrong.

"What you doing back, mister?" she wanted to know. "Darlene said you was gone for good."

"Did you say that, darlin'?"

I nodded.

"Well negatory on that. I'm here, am I not?" Then he turned to Sammy. "I hope you're not planning on drinking that." I could tell he was glad to see Sammy, whom he'd always hailed as "a good kid." He hadn't really looked at me yet. He didn't seem to notice that I'd cut off all my hair, and that I was wearing the boyish overalls he hated. It occurred to me that he also didn't know that I'd gotten my period while he was gone, and that my latest battle with Mom was over the fact that I refused to wear a bra. When I saw Dad looking at Sammy like he might just adopt him, I felt an urge to tell him that I'd rather be a Sammy than a Darlene any day, and that I'd be happy to play the son.

"Ever since the hurricane we got no running water," Sammy said. "Everybody on the street's using your pool water to flush their toilets."

"Are they now," Dad said.

"Celia's been trying to charge us for it, a nickel a bucket, but her mama won't let her," Sammy said.

"That's not all," Elaine said. "Celia and Gracie, they been coming over with caramel apples they made while their mama was at work. They been selling them apples for a quarter. Mama says those caramel wraps are only ten cents a piece at the Delchamps, but she buys them anyways because the girls got to make a living somehow."

Suddenly I felt embarrassed of the way we'd been living without him, like poor people, but at the same time I felt proud of the schemes we had come up with. "We don't need a man around to take care of things," Mom had said the day after he left. It made me feel good to know that she was right.

Dad winked at Elaine. "You tell your mother they're doing just fine. Tell her I've been sending them money."

Elaine looked at Dad like he'd told a lie. Then she said to her brother, "Let's go." Sammy obeyed, taking one of the jugs and trotting along behind her. Elaine stepped over a fallen limb and turned to us. "Mama wouldn't make that stuff up."

EIGHT YEARS LATER I'm sitting across the table from Dad at a Quincy's off Route 173 in Texas. I haven't seen either of my parents since the night I showed up in their driveway with Beth at my side and announced I was going to live with her in Bandera.

Dad's eating his steak medium. Mine is rare. He looks at my plate and asks if I'd like some meat with that blood. He says Mom is worried and prays for me every day. He says they're both trying to understand what I'm doing. "We still love you," he says, slicing his steak into bite-sized pieces. "But there are laws of nature. Maybe you just haven't met the right guy."

"I never will."

He asks me if I'm happy, if I need money, if I've met Beth's parents.

"Yes, no, yes," I answer, swishing a potato wedge around in the juice. "And while we're being forthright, there's something I've always wanted to ask you."

"Shoot."

"What did you do when you left that summer? Where did you go?"

He puts his fork down. "That's old news," he says.

"It's new news if I've never heard it."

He waves the waitress over and asks for more sweet iced tea. He squeezes the lemon wedge and stirs it around so hard the ice dissolves into little slivers. He takes a few bites of his salad, and finally says, "Promise you won't tell?"

I nod. Knowing him, the story will be only about seventy-five percent true. In his version he'll appear almost archetypal, a simple man set against impossible temptations. When my sisters and I were kids, he used to gather us in the living room on Friday nights and tell us strange stories from his past. As an air traffic controller in the Navy, he had traveled the world on a giant boat called the *Enterprise*. He claimed to have caught the fast silver planes with his bare hands, then set them gently down on the tarmac of the ship. He told us about eating monkey stew in Thailand and meeting slender showgirls in Saigon, and how he resisted those girls by closing his eyes and thinking of our mother. The stories always had some moral, which we were supposed to figure out ourselves, but more often than not the stories inspired in me a wild desire to sin, to do everything the Sunday school teachers told me I shouldn't.

"That was the year Baby was born," he begins. "All of the sudden, there she was, all pink and clean and in her crib. You girls adored her. There was your Aunt Lucy to help out. I wasn't needed. I bought a truck for three hundred dollars and drove it out to San Francisco, spent the summer with a guy I'd known on the *Enterprise*. Jim was thirty years old and divorced, no kids. When I arrived on his doorstep that summer, he asked me why I'd want to go and leave your mother."

"I always wondered the same thing," I say. "You two seemed happy enough."

Dad spears a mushroom, then puts his fork down without eating it. "I'll tell you what I told Jim, even though it may not sound like a very good excuse. Money was tight. I had more kids than I knew what to do with. And besides, I didn't really feel that I'd left y'all. I'd just taken a hiatus.

"Jim introduced me to this girl named Cindy from San Rafael. Cindy had big legs and blonde hair and nothing in the world to worry about. I borrowed Jim's convertible one night and took Cindy from San Rafael for a drive up Highway One. While we were driving,

I thought about the studio apartment your mother and I had kept in the Richmond for a few months when I was stationed in San Francisco, and the bed that folded out of the wall. I remembered taking the ferry with her across the Bay to Sausalito, and I remembered the white lipstick she used to wear, and how it took on this strange silver light against the bright blue of the San Francisco sky at night."

Something crashes in the kitchen, but Dad doesn't seem to notice. I lean forward to hear him over the noise.

"Cindy and I had steaks and beer at The Chart House, then climbed up the cliff beside the restaurant to look out at the Pacific. It was the craziest ocean I'd ever seen. The Gulf of Mexico makes you feel easy, like you could sit back and relax and fall asleep and maybe wake up in the morning with the sun on your face. But the Pacific looks like it could eat you up, like one step in the wrong direction and you'd be at the mercy of the ocean."

I imagine Dad standing above the waves with Cindy, and I think of those waves crashing over them, pulling them over the edge of the cliff, knocking them against the rocks like tin cans. I imagine their two bodies washing up together, pale and bloated, on some distant beach. And I wonder how Mom would have broken the news to Celia, Gracie, and me—whether she would have mentioned the body of Cindy from San Rafael.

"Cindy tugged me toward the water," Dad continues. "She wanted to put her feet in. The moon wasn't quite full. Cindy's hair, I realized, was not blonde so much as it was a very pale shade of brown. The air smelled of fish and steak and beer. I took my hand away and put my arm around Cindy's waist and tried to kiss her. She wouldn't let me. I thought about your mother, how she wouldn't let me the first time, but after that it was all easy and clean, like kissing me was the most natural and right thing in the world. I thought about how I should be missing her, since she was my first love and the mother of my four girls, but no amount of remembering could make me really miss her. Not the way I did in the beginning, when we were just married and I was out on the *Enterprise*, and she was waiting for me back in San Francisco."

Dad doesn't know what Mom has told us girls—how she left San Francisco while he was at sea, certain that her marriage was a mistake. He doesn't know that she stayed gone for several weeks, and that it was only Grandmother's admonition that made her go back to him.

The waitress comes over to check on us. She has dyed black hair and spindly legs and is edging up on sixty. She lingers a bit too long at our table. She wants to know where we came from and where we're going. She tells my father he should drop in again on his way back to Alabama. "I work weekdays ten to four," she says. "Saturdays I pull a double."

"I'll be here," Dad says, but the waitress and I both know he's just being polite. As soon as she steps away he's talking about Cindy again, as if he'd just been with her yesterday. "She pulled away from me and picked her way down the rocks. Just a few feet below her was a sign that said CAUTION: INTERMITTENT WAVES OF UNUSUAL SIZE AND FORCE. I pointed out the sign to her and told her to watch out, but she just looked up at me and laughed. I didn't know what else to do, so I followed her. The wind picked up and blew her flimsy skirt at crazy angles. A little farther toward the water there was another warning: PEOPLE HAVE BEEN SWEPT FROM THESE ROCKS AND DROWNED. The wooden sign kept getting jerked around by the wind; it looked like it might plunge into the ocean any minute.

"I wouldn't go any farther. Cindy made some comment about Southern boys not being so tough. Then she put her arms around my neck. We kissed for a long time out there in the cold Pacific air. I had a hard time keeping my balance. It occurred to me that we might actually fall off the rocks and into the ocean. It didn't seem like such a bad way to go. She felt so alive beneath her dress, so warm. She was a big girl, nothing frail about her. I thought about how, if I went to bed with her, she might suffocate me with her strong arms and big thighs. I wanted to pull her down right there on the rocks and make love to her. But she pulled me down first. She was wearing some strange girdle I couldn't get her out of. She had to stand up to unfasten it, and while she was doing that I thought, 'This is my chance to do the right thing. Right now I could just get up and walk back to the car.'"

"Did you?" I ask, expecting to hear the moral of the story, how he straightened his tie and took Cindy by the arm and said, "I best be getting you home."

"I'd been married for thirteen years," he says. "Thirteen faithful years. I couldn't believe a girl like Cindy could want me. Let's face it, I knew I'd never get another chance like that."

I imagine Cindy freed from her girdle, her thighs shaking slightly in the wind, a thick line of muscle snaking up each leg, and my father beneath her, awestruck. I am oddly drawn to Cindy, her solid weight and fearlessness, and I wonder if I would have the willpower to resist a woman like her.

Dad pours some Tabasco sauce on the steak he's hardly touched, catches my eye, and says, "You sure you want to hear the rest of this?"

"Are you kidding? This is the best story you've ever told." I don't tell him that I'm not sure how much of it I believe. In his stories he lives the life of a slightly different man, someone freer and more brazen. In his stories he becomes the father he thinks his daughters would have wanted, a father who makes mistakes not so different from our own. In his real life he has been a deacon and a husband, a man who never strayed too far or long from home, but in his finest stories he answers instinct over duty, passion over protocol.

"I drove back down the coast with my hand on her leg," he says. "I felt guilty for being in such a good mood, driving down the coast like that with this fun girl at my side, when at that very moment the hurricane was headed toward Alabama. We kept hearing about it on the radio. I knew your mother would have done everything she was supposed to do: boarded up the windows and tucked you all into the closet of our bedroom. She would be in the closet with you, flashlights blazing while the wind whipped outside. The wooden porch swing would be smashing against the side of the house. Your mother would be holding Baby. Celia would be reading a Nancy Drew mystery. Gracie would be nervous, trying to wedge herself between Celia and your mother, vying for her mother's attention. You'd be complaining that you didn't want to sit in the closet, that you'd rather go outside and watch the hurricane."

He's right. We did weather the storm in the closet. But I can't remember what I was doing, how I occupied my hands, if indeed I was angry to be in that confined space with my mother and sisters, hiding. I do remember thinking that we could die, that the house might collapse around us and that my father would find us, five corpses piled together amid the shoes and plastic hangers.

"I didn't take Cindy home that night. The next morning Jim came into the living room where Cindy and I had slept on a mattress on the floor. He just walked right in and stood over us and said, 'You better come look at the TV.' The three of us drank instant coffee and watched the hurricane coverage. Dauphin Island had been leveled. Seaweed littered the beach, mangled boards drifted in the shallows, and piers that had been half-ripped from their moorings hung willy-nilly over the water. The wind had razed the little houses that used to stand on wooden stilts along the beachfront. In Mobile, there were whole streets where the roofs had been ripped off. Downtown, people climbed through busted-out store windows and walked away with televisions and radios.

"I called home but the lines were dead, so I just got in the truck and started driving. I intended to make the whole distance without even stopping at a motel, because it seemed wrong to sleep without knowing what had happened to y'all. I pulled off at a rest stop near the Rio Grande, thinking to shut my eyes for ten minutes, and woke up three hours later with a vicious sunburn that cut a diagonal path across my face. I lived those two days on coffee and candy bars, and I've never felt so nervous as I did driving alone through the desert to see if I still had a house, and if I still had a wife.

"When I got home, the place seemed deserted. A limb from the big oak was blocking the front door, so I went around back. The back door was open. For a second it scared me. I had this crazy notion that maybe somebody had just walked in and taken my family."

"I was outside when you got there," I correct him. "I was selling pool water to the Sousa kids, remember? You talked to me before you ever went inside."

"No," he says. "I know for sure there was nobody around. I remember it like it was last week. I wandered in, real quiet. Part of me expected to find the place emptied out, all of you gone, and another part of me expected to find you all going about your business like I'd never left. I guess I wanted to catch my family in a candid moment, so I could know for once what your lives were like without me.

"Then I saw your mother. She was sitting at the kitchen table with Celia and Gracie, playing dominoes. I felt a momentary relief, like a big *if* had been lifted off of me, like I'd come this close to losing everything, but instead I'd lost nothing. Baby was in her high chair, and she had creamed carrots all over her. Your mother looked up. Her hair had grown and it fell across her face. She looked beautiful and kind of messy, more like the easygoing girl I had fallen in love with than the overworked wife and mother who more often than not turned away when I tried to kiss her. She must have read my mind, because she reached up and touched her hair and said, 'I've been meaning to get it cut.'"

"How does she wear it now?" I ask. The question comes from nowhere. Dad looks surprised, and I'm embarrassed for asking it.

"Shoulder length," he answers. "Kind of wavy."

I wonder if Mom will ask him the same question about me. I can imagine her face going easy and soft when Dad tells her that my crew cut has grown out, that my hair falls past my chin now. "Then

INTERMITTENT WAVES OF UNUSUAL SIZE AND FORCE

maybe she's getting over this thing," she might say, and he'll nod his head in agreement, even though he must know by now it isn't true.

"She misses you," he says, and I know he's waiting for me to give him some message of hope to take back to her, something that will make her sleep easy, but I can't think of anything to say.

"Anyway, when I walked in, Celia came over and wrapped her skinny arms around my legs; I don't think she's ever held a grudge against anybody in her life, and she didn't hold one against me. Gracie was just sitting there staring at me. I picked her up and gave her a kiss. Your mother had given her a perm, and her hair stuck out in soft fuzzy bunches around her head. Gracie wanted to know where I'd been, so I told her I'd taken a drive, and she seemed okay with that. She tried to tell me the news of the whole summer in one breath, how she'd gotten her ears pierced at the mall and how she'd been selling caramel apples. Then she told me you'd gotten your period."

I laugh, remembering how disgusted I'd been when it happened. "I wanted to close my eyes and blink like Genie and, poof, turn myself into a boy," I say.

"I turned around and saw you standing behind me, still looking like a kid. It terrified me to think that you were capable of having children. I couldn't imagine you with a boy, going on dates and sneaking kisses by the front door when he dropped you off."

Finished with my steak, I push my plate to the edge of the table. "You lucked out," I say. "When Brett Barnum kissed me in the driveway that summer I nearly gagged. I couldn't figure out why anyone would ever kiss a boy."

My father looks at me bewildered, as if I'm some stranger. "Did you ever?"

"Ever what?"

"With a boy?"

"Once, my junior year of high school. It was horrible."

"I'm sorry," he says, and I can tell he means it.

"Were you glad you came home?" I ask, changing the subject.

"Eventually, but not right away. You were even tougher than your mother," he laughs. "You just stood there glaring at me. I felt terrified and inadequate, standing in that room surrounded by women. I envied all of you. When you had a baby or lost a baby or made love to somebody, everything would be all tied up in your body—you'd feel it at your center. I could never be connected like that. I thought of your mother the year before when she miscarried, how she bled and bled and bled. She had that blood and that pain to show her what she had lost, and she dragged me to bed every night until there was another one on the way."

It's been years since I thought of the brother I almost had, the boy who died not long before he was supposed to be born. For several months after the miscarriage, Mom's speech and movements were marked by a strange desperation. She would clutch Dad's hand at the most inopportune times—like when we were eating supper or driving home from church—and say, "We have to try again."

Dad looks down at his plate. His steak is cold. The eager waitress comes over and urges us to enjoy the complimentary dessert bar. "Want some ice cream?" Dad says, standing.

"I'll take the pecan pie."

I watch him grab a thick white plate from the stack on the dessert bar, move over to the pecan pie, and lift a big piece of it with the silver serving knife. He brings it over to me, then goes back to the bar for his ice cream. The pie is cool and dense. The sugared pecans crack under my teeth. The soft-serve machine is stuck and another waitress, this one young and chubby, comes to his aid. She stands with her shoulder touching his as she expertly maneuvers the silver lever. "That should do it," she says, as the ice cream winds into his bowl in a perfectly balanced stripe of chocolate and vanilla. My father smiles at her, that wide-open smile I've seen him bestow on my mother, on me, on each of my sisters more times than I can count. When he smiles that way he looks surprised more than anything, as if he can't

INTERMITTENT WAVES OF UNUSUAL SIZE AND FORCE

believe his good fortune at having a woman pay him such undivided attention. I imagine him smiling that way at Cindy as he speeds along the Northern California coast, his hand on her thigh, for a moment believing that he has attained that alternate life, the one he might have lived.

My father and I say goodbye in the parking lot. He hugs me as if nothing has changed. "Give my regards to Elizabeth," he says.

A few minutes later I pull up in front of our small house on the edge of town. I stand outside the kitchen window, watching Beth, but she doesn't see me. She is wearing a small gray T-shirt that says Longhorns Forever. Her hands are covered in cornmeal, her back bent over the table. I walk around to the front door, ease it open, and tiptoe into the kitchen, thinking to surprise her, but she looks up and grins. Her glasses are speckled with flour. "Trying to scare me?" she says. "How's your dad?"

"Good. He says we should visit sometime. He wants to meet you for real." This is the first time I've lied to her. I'm surprised at how easy it comes out, how natural it sounds.

I stand behind her and wrap my arms around her waist, bury my head in her neck. She smells like Texas—not the Texas of industry and cattle that we drove through to get here, but her own special Texas smell, heat and grass, faint petrol and paper bags, a smell that seems to always occupy a few feet of space around her, no matter where she is. It's nothing like the salty hot smell of Alabama's Gulf Coast, nothing like anything I knew before I met her. I slip my hand under her shirt, rest my palm on her stomach, and feel the steady pulse deep beneath her skin. Were Beth to slip away, I cannot imagine that I would be as steadfast as my mother, who did not follow my father out the front door when he left, who did not beg him to stay.

Beth turns to face me. Her hair is dusted with cornmeal. The thick black frames of her eyeglasses look comical and severe. Her back feels very small, it curves just so beneath my hands. I wrap my arms tighter around her and hold on.

Sunday

at

Red

Lobster

"*We*'ve already got three," my father said one Sunday at the Red Lobster. Darlene stared at her catfish as if she knew what was coming. Celia and I shared a plate of baby shrimp, deep-fried and smothered in ketchup.

"Maybe a boy," my mother said. She was drinking iced tea. The strings of a lemon slice floated in the brown liquid. Darlene ate a spoonful of horseradish and said she hated boys, but I was thinking it could be nice. I thought of the toys that would appear. Race cars and guns, monsters with detachable limbs. Boys said dirty words and knew terrible things that they would tell you for a price. Brothers took the blame for things girls did; my friend Angel had explained this to me. Angel had written on the walls and her brother Jimmy was spanked for it, Angel once peed on the floor and Jimmy suffered greatly. I thought it had been settled—the brother was coming, I would lead a life of disobedience devoid of consequence.

We spent that summer preparing for the boy's arrival. Mother called a family meeting to choose a name. We decided on Joshua, in honor of the man who led his ragtag army around the city of Jericho seven times under order of the Lord, the man who crumbled those mighty walls with nothing but shouts and cymbals and singing. During the months of her pregnancy our mother's small tidy body was transformed into something statuesque and sure. I laid my head against her tight round belly and listened for the joyful noise my tiny brother was surely making in honor of his namesake.

Not long before everything got bad in a way that could never be fixed, Mother told me this like a piece of advice I should remember but never tell: "Men may lead the armies, but women rule the earth."

A week later and quite unexpected, Daddy got his way but Mother was punished for it, blood like ketchup, clotted and thick, the bathroom a mess for days. In the room that smelled of ammonia, my mother said three girls weren't enough. She didn't know I was there. She had forgotten us so quickly.

Next year she did it her way. It was a sister, not a brother, who sent our father away, though he didn't stay gone for long. Still, it was a good thing, those six weeks in the summer of Hurricane Frederick, the record player going all the time and the five of us dancing together in the living room beneath the cheap chandelier.

Does Anyone

Know You

Are Going

This Way

*I*t is eight o'clock when we leave Reykjavik behind us, driving north with no sure destination. Judging from the utter absence of light, it could be midnight. Heading out into the world while it is still dark always makes me feel cheated—like those mornings in Alabama when our mother would usher me and Jimmy out of the house, still in our pajamas, and load us into the car for the six-hour ride to her sister's house in Atlanta. Laden with blankets and pillows, half-asleep, my brother and I would walk barefoot into the carport, our mother guiding us with her flashlight. Those mornings we obeyed silently, without breakfast, the previous night's fight an ugly memory surfacing as her voice called us from sleep.

It happened many times. In the dark like that, we would escape. Coasting backwards down the driveway, engine off, headlights dead, I would think of my father inside the house, oblivious in his bed, snoring softly. Leaving him, I would remember the shape of his face during sleep. His mouth was a lovely thick line I had often kissed, sneaking into their bedroom while my mother cried and cursed in some other room of the house. I would hold my hand over his mouth, feel the long, warm bursts of his breath escaping. His breath made a circle of moisture on my palm.

"Angel? Is that you?" he would say, never opening his eyes, too comfortable in his sleep to understand that we were leaving.

The car, I remember, was blue. The wide vinyl seat stretched out like a bed. Jimmy and I lay with our heads at opposite ends, our knees touching. Like my father, Jimmy could sleep with the conviction of a dead man.

My mother always seemed to envy my father's ability to sleep—to close his eyes and exit the world—while she was ever wakeful. She kept the door to their bedroom open so she could hear any disturbance in ours—an irregular breath, a dangerous-sounding cough, the practiced steps of an intruder. My mother was painfully aware of the myriad of ways in which a body could cease to function. She would rush into our room at night, having been awoken by some insignificant sound, and lean over our beds, anxious and ever-vigilant, to make certain that we were still among the living. Her breath in the night always smelled of milk, sweet and slightly sour, and her heart was so full of fear it pounded. It is possible that those predawn trips to Atlanta, and the innocent meetings with the exhausted man who waited for us in a parking lot halfway to our destination, were my mother's way of punishing my father for sleeping, for being so quiet and serene, even after a fight.

JIMMY AND I drive at a slow steady speed, trusting our headlights to guide us through the blackness. We barely talk, trading places every hour or so just so that we can get out of the car and stretch our limbs and breathe in the cold, wakeful air. Sometime between eleven o'clock and noon the sun makes its appearance, and the landscape takes shape before us—low white hills undulating beneath the orange light, here and there a geyser gushing forth in a torrent of steam, and then a cold, still body of water spotted with jagged mounds of sparkling ice.

We have just topped yet another snow-covered rise when the sign appears. Red letters on a yellow background: VARUD! VEIT EINHVER AF FERDUM PINUM HER, with the English translation below. DOES ANYONE KNOW YOU ARE GOING THIS WAY. The sign is very Icelandic in its politeness, its simple and somehow frightening fluidity. The unspoken warning, the not-so-subtle implication, is that one could easily come to the end of the line out here, freeze to death in one's car, be discovered months later during the spring thaw, stiff fingers curled around the fringe of a cheerfully patterned scarf.

We drive in silence, just us and the hum of the heater, the sound of the wind whooshing over the roof of our rented vehicle. Our tires make muddy tracks in the untouched snow. The ice caps in the distance are so white they let off a strange blue glow. I operate the stick shift while Jimmy steers with his good hand and works the foot pedals. I don't need any instruction from him. I know instinctively when to shift from second to third, when to go into overdrive. I don't have to see his foot on the clutch in order to know at exactly what moment to grip the black leather knob and push. It is almost as if his foot and my hand are parts of the same body.

Yesterday, Jimmy and I took the morning bus from Reykjavik to Blaa Lonio, a swimming pool near the small fishing village of Grindavik. I was under the mistaken impression that Blaa Lonio was a hot spring, some kind of natural paradise where one could bathe in the shadow of ice-capped mountains. Only after we arrived did I learn that the pool is actually the runoff from the Svartsengi power plant, which generates all of the heat for Grindavik with seawater that has been heated as it seeps beneath the lava. As Jimmy took my hand and led me down the steps into the pool, the vapor parted and I saw the giant stacks of the power plant juxtaposed against moss-covered lava formations. The volcanic rock on the bottom cut into my feet.

The air smelled bright and egglike. The Icelandic girls in their dark swimsuits had pale, perfect bodies that seemed iridescent when submerged beneath the sulfuric water. I was jealous of their whiteness, of the way my brother looked at them and the way their wet hair clung to their cheekbones. Their mannerisms exuded grace, their glance revealed that subtle confidence so common among island people. One girl with short black hair and blue eyes looked so wholesome and untouched, I was certain if I reached a finger forward and pressed it to her skin she would bloom, the blush spreading from the spot where I touched her to her entire body. She leaned her back against the wall of the pool and lifted her knees to the surface. The water separated around her kneecaps, while beneath the surface her whole body seemed to waver, magnified and white.

It happened, then, the way it always happens. He went to her. Their voices were muffled, but I am certain he told her his name. His head nodded in my direction and she looked at me—relieved, perhaps, to learn that I was only his sister. Within about five minutes she had fallen for him, leaning into him as if she'd known him for weeks or even months, curving her back to accept the pressure of his hand in the small of it.

My brother's power over women is absolute, a gift he has never had to work for. He can walk into a room and choose the woman he wants, direct some subtle glance her way, and she will come to him. I often wonder if it has something to do with the arm that he lost as a child, the way it makes him look vulnerable and mysterious, like a man with a tragic past. She hadn't touched the bad arm yet; they never do, not until they know him better, and then the touch is always gentle, tentative, as if the injury were fresh, the flesh around the wound still delicate.

Sometimes when Jimmy and I are driving, or sitting in front of the television, or eating, I allow my gaze to fall on the place where strangers are too polite to look. I touch it, too, the hard knob of bone over which the doctors folded the skin. His eyes close at the pleasure of it, the light touch of my fingers on the end of his arm where it tapers neatly as a sausage. Right after it happened, the white bandages were soaked with blood. Jimmy would reach over and grab the empty space, fighting with the phantom pains. The only way I could help him was to massage the amputated arm and hand. "I'm rubbing your thumb now," I would say. "The second finger, the middle." In that way I would go from finger to finger, then up to the palm of his hand, then his wrist, describing my touch on every inch of the part of himself that my brother could feel but could no longer see.

THERE WAS NO snow that day. There was never any snow in Fairhope, where it stayed uncomfortably warm right through winter.

Jimmy was eight. I was ten. He and my parents were in the blue Impala. They were coming to pick me up from my dance class. I was untying the ribbon of my left tap shoe when my brother was thrown from the car. No one could confirm this for me, but I remember a sharp jolt of pain through my arm as I was untying the shoe. Later, at the hospital, my aunt would tell me, "Your brother's arm was hurt so badly it had to be amputated." My parents were extracted from the wreckage, rushed to the hospital, and declared dead on arrival. There was no water on the roads, no potholes, no mechanical failure, no drunk driver slamming into the car that carried my family toward me, where I waited impatiently with my yellow vinyl dance bag. There existed no medical condition such as heart failure or epileptic seizure that might have caused my father to run the car off Government Boulevard into a concrete ditch.

In the ambulance, calm and collected, unaware of the absence of his arm, Jimmy told the paramedics that I was at my dance class on Schillinger Road, and that our aunt and uncle were visiting from

DOES ANYONE KNOW YOU ARE GOING THIS WAY

Atlanta and could be reached at such and such number. The paramedics called them first, and then Miss Peggy, who played Jimmy Buffet on the radio all the way to Providence Hospital, where my dead parents waited. She sang "Cheeseburger in Paradise" at the top of her lungs and asked me to sing along. My legs stuck to the vinyl seat of Miss Peggy's green truck. It was an old Ford, I remember, and the knob had come off the stick shift. There was a wadded-up washcloth where the knob was supposed to be, secured with a thick rubber band.

I have often wondered how things might have been different if the ditch had been made of dirt and grass and gravel, the yielding stuff of nature. Or if my brother had worn his seatbelt and had not been tossed—by gravity, by God, by inexplicable forces involving velocity and direction—out the side window into the soft, plush weed cover of an unkempt lawn. If the rusted metal blade of a discarded fan, converted into a garden border during some misguided home improvement project, had been positioned differently, a few inches to the left or right perhaps, and had sliced straight through some vital part instead of taking off my brother's arm.

"It wasn't an accident," Jimmy would tell me, many years after the event that we had always referred to as *the accident*. "He meant to drive us off the road. It was right after the part where he said, 'God forgive me for what I am about to do.'"

Ever since my brother told me that, my mind has been filled with questions. What did my father know? About my mother, about the man who often met us halfway between Fairhope and Atlanta, at Homer's Diner in Milstead, Alabama. This man always had bags under his eyes, and he would yawn over his coffee and apple pie, his mouth opening so wide you could see clear to the back of his throat. I always got the feeling he hadn't slept in days. We called him Mr. Evan, and we were under strict orders not to mention him to our father. I never saw Mr. Evan touch my mother in an inappropriate way. I never saw him kiss her. We would pull into the parking lot of

Homer's Diner and he would be standing there, any time of day or night, waiting. He was always wearing khaki pants, a golf shirt with some unidentifiable insignia, and black loafers that were too shiny to be leather. My mother would get out of the car and embrace him as we watched from the back seat. Sometimes she would cry into his collar, and sometimes she would laugh at something we couldn't hear. Then she would give us the nod and we would get out of the car, excited to be there at the diner that served Homer's World Famous French Toast. "Hi, Mr. Evan," Jimmy would say, acting as if none of it was any big deal. Meanwhile, I would eye the man suspiciously; but no matter how hard I tried, I could never work up any anger toward him.

The curse of tragic beginnings is that nothing in your life after that is capable of conveying any sense of drama. When the one defining moment of your life happens early on, when at the age of ten you are told that your parents have been killed, everything thereafter is like a punch line delivered long after the joke is over. You live your entire life with a sense that the timing is all off. There is no driving force to move you forward, as it is impossible to imagine that any event can equal the impact of that first horrible moment.

The difference between me and Jimmy is that I am resigned, content to pass my days in quiet routine. I work at a nursery in Fairhope, just a five-minute drive from the house where we grew up and a half-mile from Miss Peggy's Dance Studio. Peggy Ward still owns the school, but she no longer teaches there. Every now and then she stops in for an African violet or an aloe plant, something small and easily cared for, something that does not require more love than she can give. Every December without fail she purchases ten chrysanthemums, the pots wrapped in shimmery green foil. She always asks if I'm getting along okay, her eyes tearing up, as if twenty years have not passed since the day she drove me to the hospital and escorted me to the waiting room and stood tugging at the shoulders of her leotard, not sure what to do with herself, while my aunt told me that my parents were dead. Miss Peggy stood beside my uncle, who was slumped in an orange chair, weeping in a way I had never seen a man weep. He wore socks of two different colors, and I noticed for the first time that he was more handsome than my father. He looked up at me but did not seem to see me, and in the following years, living with him and my aunt in the big house they bought on Delancey Street a few months after the accident, I felt less like their inherited child than like a thought at the back of their minds, a mental presence they could never shake. Sometimes my uncle would look up from the television and seem startled to find me sitting in the room with him, and he would say, "Come here," and I would go to him. "How are things?" he would ask, trying, I think, to be fatherly.

Somewhere along the line, Miss Peggy gained weight and developed a nervous disorder that makes her head shake, and it is strange to see her that way, the once-graceful woman who taught me how to demi-plié, shaking and teary-eyed, looking awkward in her too-tight jeans. The day she took me to the hospital she didn't seem sad, just confused; and I can't help but wonder if the pity she displays now is her way of making up for her cheerfulness on the day my parents died, a self-imposed penance for that soulful rendition of "Cheeseburger in Paradise."

I often work alone after hours in the nursery's greenish light, transferring flowers to small terra-cotta pots, cringing at the fibrous ripping of roots when I am not careful enough. It is comforting to be involved in the lives of things, the simple sturdy patterns of growth and germination—soothing to know that the cycles of sleep and awakening are beyond my control, inalterable, determined by the steady arrival of the seasons.

Jimmy, on the other hand, has spent his life searching for some adventure that will outshine our parents' death—something grander or more shocking, or even more horrifying—some moment that will overshadow that early brush with reality. He has yet to find it. He is forever traveling, jumping from one job to the next, disappearing for months at a time without telling me where he has gone. He is open to any legend or superstition, any story that promises an experience unlike the ones he has already known. That's why we're driving across Iceland in January, pushing our rented four-wheel drive over roads that are not meant to be traveled this time of year, heading in the general direction of the three ragged peninsulas that jut into the Arctic Ocean on the island's north central coast. "I'm taking you to the top of the world," Jimmy said back in Fairhope, placing his finger at this precise place on the globe.

"On one of these peninsulas, Skagi, there is a series of low gravel hills overlooking a bog called Gullbrekka," Jimmy tells me as we drive. "There was once a farm there, inhabited by several families and an impressive number of sheep. Hundreds of years ago, the farm and its inhabitants sank into the bog, a miniature Atlantis." He has heard that there are ghosts there, that the hills are haunted by the soggy spirits of children and sheep who sank, shrieking, into the mud and gravel.

YESTERDAY, AFTER Blaa Lonio, we took the 3:00 bus to Reykjavik— me and Jimmy and the beautiful girl. It was warm inside the bus. The seats were wide and thickly cushioned, the windows clean. The big wheels held us high off the ground, and I watched the smooth black road skirting beneath us. No one spoke. The sun had just begun to set. The quality of light was unlike any I had seen, soft and somehow miraculous, flowing like liquid over the moonlike landscape. There was not much snow along the coast road that ran between Keflavic and Reykjavik—just undulating mounds of black volcanic rock, dusted with white powder.

Beneath us, volcanoes boiled and bubbled. It is alarming to think that this country, which seems so content in its aloofness, its separation from the rest of the world, is ultimately at the mercy of some two hundred volcanoes whose craters have simmered beneath it for thousands of years, their vents buried deep in the frigid sea. They are time bombs, sure and simple, and the question is not whether they will erupt, but when. I thought of the story Jimmy told me of the Vikings in the valley of Thjorsardalur, whose farms were buried under tons of volcanic ash. Eight hundred years later, Scandinavian archeologists uncovered what was left of the smothered Saga-age farms. I imagined the hardy Vikings living in the shadow of snow-capped Hekla, constructing their collective houses, completely unaware that the mountain would one day bury them.

My brother and the girl sat in front of me. Through the space between our seats, I could see the small white circles her breath left on the clean window glass. She was staring out, her head turned away from him. She was not smiling or frowning but rather seemed expressionless, her face as empty and lovely as a mannequin beneath her blue knit cap. My brother had slipped his hand through the opening in her coat and she allowed it to rest on her thigh. I am stunned over and over again by the quick intimacy he forms with women: the way he can rest his hand on the leg of a girl he met only hours ago and she will not reject him, as if he has a right, as if his hand belongs there.

It is a disconcerting thing to enter a new place in the darkness, with no sense of your surroundings. Until you experience a place in daylight you are entirely at its mercy; it is always for you like a dream, impenetrable. Now, approaching the city at sundown, I saw it for the first time in the falling light and wished, immediately, that it had remained a mystery. The houses and apartments at the outskirts of the capital were white and angular. The arrangement of them, the unforgiving, utilitarian shapes, seemed sadly suburban.

We all got off at the Hotel Saga, where Jimmy and I were staying. "We're going for a walk," Jimmy said to me, as we stood shivering on the doormat. "Would you like to come?"

Certain that Jimmy only invited me out of duty, I declined and went up to our room. I spent the evening writing letters. I wrote one to our aunt, who couldn't understand why we were coming here, and to Grace, whom I haven't seen in five years. *Where are you these days? Have you married? Is Ivan still in the picture?* We had coffee together soon after she finished college, but we couldn't find the right questions to ask each other, much less the appropriate answers. She knows me too well for me to be easy with her. Years before, I had told her everything about that night behind Dreamland Skating Rink. We had lain on her bed, staring up at the ceiling, while I described the referee's hands clenched around my neck, the aluminum siding of the building cold against my back, the gravel that stuck to my legs after he went back inside to work, and I lay there not knowing what to do, hearing the disco music thundering through the walls, "Jive Talkin'" by the Bee Gees. My aunt and uncle wanted me to keep the baby. Grace convinced me otherwise. She was in the waiting room in the clinic when it was done. I cannot see her without thinking of the doctor in his light blue frock, the cold metal of the stirrups against my feet. In my letter, I wrote a page and a half about Iceland, about how Jimmy showed up from out of the blue one afternoon and said, "You have to go with me." I addressed the envelope to her parents' house. The last time I saw her she was moving to New York to be with Ivan, but she could be anywhere by now.

By midnight Jimmy had not returned. I thought of him out there in the cold night with the pale Icelandic girl. Perhaps he had taken her down by the ocean, along the dark pier where the colorful fishing boats docked. I stayed awake all night, staring out our wide picture window, then at our empty bed, then back out the window again. Across the street from our hotel stood a church, austere and gleaming. From its roof rose a giant neon cross that blazed white and anomalous in the darkness, its ethereal light pulsing over the icy road. That single source of light contained itself so completely, selfishly almost, that the darkness beyond it seemed absolute, rendering the nearby sea invisible. The cross reminded me of the steeple on top of Bay View Baptist Church. I went with Grace sometimes when we were children. I used to marvel at the calmness of the Baptist services, the somber timbre of their hymns, the low drone of the preacher's voice as he lulled us into prayer. Their worship was so unlike the wild services at the little church by the bay in Fairhope, where grown ups danced and shouted and spoke in tongues, where my father's eyes rolled back in his head and he became a different man. My mother explained it this way: "Baptists don't get the Holy Spirit."

Jimmy returned at seven in the morning, his cheeks flushed from the cold. I watched him undress, and in that oddly religious light he looked almost Icelandic: blue-eyed and pale skinned, his blonde hair sticking out in all directions. He is the most chameleonesque person I know, able to take on the look and customs of just about any place he visits, be it New York City or Arkansas or Budapest. Everywhere he goes, tourists stop him to ask directions. He can spend a couple of days in any place, among any people, and look like someone who belongs. I, on the other hand, feel always like the proverbial stranger in a strange land.

When I think of my childhood home I think not of the small yellow house in Fairhope, or of the restored plantation home on Delancey where we were raised by our aunt and uncle after our parents died. I think, instead, of some spot on the highway between Fairhope and Atlanta—some unfixed point between the house where my father slept and the house where my mother's sister waited. When I think of home I think of the blue Impala with its big antenna, and of my mother in the front seat, crying. The radio is on but you know she isn't really listening, because often it's just noise, static crackling in the darkness. Jimmy is snoring softly, a good noise that reassures me. Like my father, he is always sleeping. When, for a moment, his snoring subsides, my mother looks back to make sure that he is still breathing. "Is everything okay, Angel?" she whispers, and I say yes, and I feel that we are two women alone in the world. She asks would I like some pumpkin pie. She doesn't mean it, it's just a thing she says. I say that I would like some pumpkin pie before I die, and that cheers her up for a moment, and I know that there is something between us, then, that Jimmy will never have. When I sit up and gaze out the back window, I see the lights of other cars approaching, passing us, moving forward in the empty dark.

IT IS SIX IN the evening, and the sky is black as midnight. Upon reading the warning—DOES ANYONE KNOW YOU ARE GOING THIS WAY—I suggest we turn around and spend the night in the village a few miles back.

"I'm sure there's another town up the road," Jimmy says. He lifts his foot off the gas to swerve around a clump of ice, and I shift down to second. "Trust me," he says. "Have I ever failed you?"

He has a point. Jimmy and I have made these lengthy drives before. The landscape is new, but the routine is familiar. We have set out, dozens of times, from some town or city that Jimmy has chosen to live in for a little while. We always begin with him behind the wheel, me in the passenger seat, the map spread over my lap. We have stayed in run-down motels in places like Loving, Texas, Bucksnort, Tennessee, and Monte Rio, California. On many occasions we have shared a bed, our thighs touching beneath the musty blankets, and I have stayed awake—fearful of the faulty locks, the unsavory guests—while Jimmy slept a deep and restful sleep.

YOU GROW UP with a man and you don't know him. It takes a while to realize that. When I think of my father I think of him dancing, all filled up with the Holy Spirit in the little church by the bay in Fairhope. Or I think of his mouth, the soft line of it while he is sleeping. I think of the circles his breath makes on my open palm, and of the occasional rowdy anger, his fist puncturing a window, blood running down his hand. He never goes for us. We know, with him, that

126

we are safe, and that our mother is safe, because it's always our father who ends up wounded. He will only hurt himself.

"Has he always been sad?" I ask my mother. We are in the car when I ask this. Jimmy is sleeping. She is looking at me in the rearview mirror. Like that we talk, one reflection to another. In this manner, it is almost as if she is not talking to her nine-year-old daughter. And so she is able to tell me things she wouldn't say if we were face to face.

"Yes. He has a chemical imbalance. He won't take his medication."

"Are you sad?"

"Sometimes."

"Why?"

"I don't want to be with your father anymore."

I ask her then, for the first and only time, if she wants to be with Mr. Evan. It takes her a long time to answer. I begin to worry, but then she says, "Mr. Evan and I are friends, honey. We've known each other for years. We have a lot in common."

You try to picture them as separate people, not together. You try to think of your mother not with your father, or your father not with your mother. The very thought is so senseless it makes you laugh, just as a pair of headlights rises up over the hill in the oncoming lane. Maybe it's your laughter, maybe the shock of the lights, but your mother is herself again, and she says, "Oh, it's nothing, I'm just talking." She concentrates on the road and you concentrate on her hair, rising mysterious and dark above her head. You know that she will carefully remove the long silver pins from her hair, one at a time, right when you pass under the sign on the highway that says MIL-STEAD 2 MILES. Her hair, which usually stands high and severe—*a woman's crown* the preacher says—will fall in soft waves around her shoulders, down her back. Before easing into the parking lot of the diner she will stop on the side of the road, reach into her small black

DOES ANYONE KNOW YOU ARE GOING THIS WAY

purse, and pull out a silver tube. Looking in the rearview mirror, she will apply the soft orange lipstick, and she doesn't have to say, "Don't tell your father." It is against all the rules of the church, this makeup and this hair, and you love her for looking this way.

You grow up with a man, you don't know him. A father will never tell you such things as a mother will tell you. He is closed to you, a secret. Waking or sleeping, or in the car in the dark and leaving, you can't know him.

When I think of my uncle I think of him slumped in that orange chair in the hospital, weeping and defeated. I think of him standing in the kitchen of his big house on Delancey, his arms around his wife, my mother's sister, his hands moving across her back. She is wearing a rose-colored blouse. His hands have lifted the blouse, her skin beneath it is pale and freckled. Her back yields to him, bending, she is saying something I can't hear. I pretend they are my parents, that he is my father and she is my mother, that they have always loved each other this way, that she never screamed at him and he never ran her into a ditch.

It seems we are always leaving their house or coming to their house, always in between.

You grow up with a man and you don't know what he will do in an emergency situation, how he will behave in a snowdrift. It is five past midnight when we begin skidding, and there's no telling whose fault it is. We are in agreement that there was some miscalculation, a miscommunication between his foot and my hand. When we hit the ice his foot met the accelerator, because it is a fact tried and proven that one should not break when forced into a skid. Breaking is instinctual, but the laws of physics tell you to tap the accelerator lightly, to drive out of the skid rather than fighting it. I am not a practitioner of physics. Jimmy accelerates and hits the clutch. Meanwhile, I shift down. We are swerving for several surprising moments, sliding uncontrollably. All I can think of is the Mad Hatter ride at Disney World, and Jimmy throwing up in our magic teacup. We are not injured, only stuck, several yards off the road, surrounded by an indescribable quiet.

"What do we do now?"

"Put us in first," Jimmy says. I do so. He steps on the accelerator and we jerk forward slightly. After that, the tires whir ineffectually in the snow. Our Range Rover came with a tool kit including shovel and crowbar, so we take turns digging the snow from behind the tires, then try unsuccessfully to back out again.

"We need something to use for traction," Jimmy says cheerfully, always happy to meet a challenge. We settle on the floor mats, wedge them under the rear tires, and try once again to back out. This goes on for quite some time, until Jimmy announces that he's going for help.

"There's no one out there. You'll freeze to death."

"What do you suggest?"

"Let's wait out the night. Maybe someone will drive by tomorrow."

"You heard the guy back at the gas station," Jimmy says. "No one uses these roads in winter."

"I'm not going out there."

"Of course not. You stay with the car. There's no reason for both of us to freeze to death." He's laughing when he says this, but I am struck suddenly by an image of him frozen in place as he walks, the knees bent in ambulatory motion like the victim of a volcanic eruption. I imagine that hundreds of years from now archaeologists will discover him walking away from me, and nearby they'll find "a young female" curled inside a piece of obsolete machinery. These physical fragments will be used to piece together a story in which Jimmy and I are the tragic hero and heroine. Like the Vikings in the valley of Thjorsardalur or the Gullbrekka farmers, we will disappear, unnoticed in our own time only to be made legends in another.

Jimmy puts his good arm around me, rests the other on my shoulder, and plants a big kiss on my mouth. His lips are cold, so dry they stick to mine, and we stand this way for several moments, locked in an awkward embrace. I wonder what it would feel like to be kissed by him the way the Icelandic girl was kissed by him. I have a craving to feel the warmth inside his mouth. It seems that something momentous should happen between us now, something that each of us can cling to years from now if the other doesn't make it. I've always wished I had experienced that with my parents—one last piggyback ride from my father on the morning of the day he drove my family into a ditch, a few final words of advice and encouragement from my mother before she died. I lift my face and moisten my lips with my tongue, thinking to kiss Jimmy the way other girls have kissed him, but he just looks at me as if I've gone loony and begins to pull away. The silk of my coat rubs against his suede, making slippery noises.

Then he is walking away from me, into the limitless dark. The right sleeve of his coat dangles, empty halfway down. There is nothing defeated in his posture. He walks energetically, despite the fact that he didn't go to bed last night. Maybe all the years of sleep have steeled him for this night; perhaps he has stored up so much of it that he could stay awake indefinitely. His figure disappears and only the sound of him reaches me, his boots crunching on the snow. I know what is going on in his head. He is thinking that this is an adventure, the one he's been waiting for all his life.

"How long will you be gone?" I shout. There is not even the comfort of an echo. My voice dissipates in the wide, invisible whiteness. I climb into the Range Rover, lock the doors, and curl up in the backseat with the wool blanket we bought in Reykjavik. I am wearing several layers, plus a wool hat and gloves and scarf. It isn't enough. There's no getting warm.

I think of my father in those final moments, the car careening toward the ditch, the hood crashing into the cement wall and crunching inward. As the windshield shatters does he think of me, of my tennis shoes poised on the curb outside Miss Peggy's Dance Studio, waiting? Does he turn toward my mother and see her face, that last long look of surprise, and wish there were time to get the car back on the road, to retract the thing he has done? I wonder if he is aware, as his skull plows through the windshield and smacks against the cement, of the miraculous way in which my brother is thrown from the car, so that only my parents will die there together, alone with the anger they have cultivated through the years. Perhaps he is simply thinking that it is time to go to sleep.

My dreams are cold and vivid. I dream of the ghosts who are said to wander the rims of dormant craters, like circus performers balancing on the jagged ledges above deep pools of green, and of Jimmy out there among them, embracing them, each one an icy apparition that melts in the heat of his hands.

It is almost five in the morning when I wake, shaking, feeling frozen to the bone. I crawl into the front seat and turn the ignition. The engine emits a weak, sputtering sound. I try again and again, panicked, and finally hear a dull rumble beneath the hood. I turn the heater on and cold air blasts through the vents. Slowly it begins to warm.

There is no sign of Jimmy. Snow has begun to swirl around me, blanketing the car. I turn on the wipers to clear the windshield, but they stick, beating against the crystalline layers. I shine the headlights out into the snow, put it in first, and try, without success, to pull out of the snowdrift. There is nothing, just empty space and me, and the cold, and beneath us, somewhere, the hot lava of the volcanoes bubbling, boiling, waiting to erupt. I drift in and out of sleep, thinking of the redness of the lava, and of buried cities in distant places, bodies frozen in motion. You see it on television, strange photographs in magazines, and the bodies look cold beneath the whitened ash, snowbound almost, but you know that they were burning. Sometimes their eyes were open at the moment of death—vigilant and wakeful, like Lot's wife—and I wonder what it is like to see the flow moving toward you, inevitable, that fiery heat descending.

A hard wind starts up from the west. It beats against the car, rocking me back and forth. I tell myself that Jimmy is fine, that he has stumbled upon a house. He has found some gorgeous Icelandic girl, bright-eyed and firm of bone, in whose kitchen he sits, warming by the stove. She feeds him smoked salmon and cheese, steaming mugs of cocoa. Perhaps she is wearing a skirt that rides up over the pink of her knees, and he cannot resist the soft blurry heat of her, and when they are done he will come to me. I envision him unbuttoning her blouse, loosening her bra, sliding his hands over the whiteness of her breasts. Her nipples respond to him, hardening beneath his fingertips. She leads him to another room, where a small bed waits. The bed is piled with heavy blankets and soft, down-filled comforters. She allows him to undress her. For a moment they stand apart, not touching; he notices that her skin shimmers like the silken belly of a fish. *Wait*, he says, *don't move*, wanting to remember this image, so he can tell me later. He follows her into the bed, and the weight of the blankets combined with the warmth of her body pulls him down into sleep. It is a good and peaceful sleep. When he wakes he will remember; he will come to me.

Seven A.M. Not a single car has passed. I have trudged around the car six times, trying to get the blood going. I leave the car on for heat. By 10:00 I have run the gas down to empty. I embark upon a search for food within the confines of the automobile, throwing our backpacks and maps and travel guides into a great disorder. Then I devour two squares of Hershey bar that I find between the back seat cushions. I finish off the bottled water and feel thankful for the snow and remember the Bible verse, *Drink and you shall never thirst*.

Once in Vermont, when we were children, we gathered new snow in a pan and poured maple syrup on it. The snow turned crusty and sweet. Our mother was listening to Johnny Mathis on her portable radio. Our father was inside the lodge, alone. We had been instructed not to speak to him. Earlier, of course, there had been an unpleasant spectacle. My mother had said, "The kids and I are leaving you. This time I mean it." My father, not believing her, had gone to bed in his underwear. I walked into their room and saw him

climbing beneath the thick comforter, looking somehow dimin-
ished without his clothes. He caught me watching him.

"Your mother has found someone else," he said.

I asked, "Why won't you take your medicine?" The way I remember it there was no gentleness in my voice, no element of filial
concern. I said it as an accusation against this man who was always
sad and always sleeping, this man whose moods could not be de-
pended upon.

"Do you love me?" he asked.

I didn't answer him. All I could think was that if he would take his
medicine we wouldn't have to leave him. If he would just take his
medicine our mother would love him properly and Mr. Evan would-
n't wait for us in a dusty parking lot in Milstead, standing there
weary-eyed and patient in his black plastic loafers. We could end our
night drives to Atlanta, our furtive visits with that dull, kind man. If
my father would just take his medicine we wouldn't have to see our
uncle's face when we arrived at the door of his house in Atlanta, and
we wouldn't have to answer the same old questions that he asked
every time because he didn't know how to talk to children. "Is it hot
in Alabama?" our uncle used to ask. "Do you like school? Would
you like a chipped beef sandwich?"

By 11:15 the light begins to break, a strange and liquid northern
light moving over the top of the world. In the distance I see a vehicle
moving toward me, a good shape rising out of the whiteness. I try to
open the door, but it is now frozen shut. I sit sideways and ram
against it with my feet until it gives, opening with a loud crack, a shattering of icicles, a crumbling away of accumulated frost. I climb out
of the Range Rover, sinking knee-deep in the snow. I wave my arms
and shout, feeling elated, overwhelmed with relief and gratitude.
The vehicle stops. Someone gets out of it and begins walking toward
me. It is my brother. He has not forgotten. He has come for me.

O-lama-lama-ana-bacha-sabbatine-wyo. My own voice fills the air,
fluid and strange and sweet, a memory from those mornings at the

little church by the beach in Fairhope, my father shouting out while sweat rolls down his face, the drum of the tambourine cool against my palm, my mother's hands held high above her, shouting praises to the Lord. *O-lama-lama*. Gracie is dancing with me. Later there will be cake of such a deep red you'll almost believe the cake is bleeding. *Bacha-sabbatine-wyo*. There is joy in it, and heat, a warmth shooting all through my body, electricity, pain. It is something close to a prayer, these strange sounds I send up, believing for a moment that my parents are watching, that they can hear me, that they have brought him back to me.

Faith

*H*ere is what my mother told me the year she taught Sunday school, the year we spent Saturdays at the Baptist Book Store on Demopolis Way: "With the faith of just one mustard seed you can move a mountain."

"Baloney," Darlene said when I told her the news.

"It's in the Bible," I argued. I imagined our mother sucking on a mustard seed, standing in front of Red Mountain in Birmingham and willing it to move. Surely there would be a great rumbling, followed by untold disaster, as the fifty-three foot tall Vulcan atop the mountain pitched forward and crushed the city with his cast iron fist. Then the police would show up and arrest my mother for vandalism.

My mother believes that her faith in God, or more likely her faith in her own womanly powers, has moved my father to sanity. In truth, he was more fun the old way, before he succumbed to reason.

I remember nights at our house on Epson Downs Street, when I would hear a noise in my bedroom and wake to find my father standing before the bed, wearing his purple housecoat, arms stiff at his side. In my half-sleep, he resembled some dancing ghost, a velvet apparition waltzing before my bed.

In his hand he held the gun. I would look up at his face, that face gone wild with love and fear. The streetlamp through the thin pink curtains on my window lit him up, something like my father and something like what my mother said he was, a man obsessed. He was looking for the person he had heard roaming the house.

I have three sisters, but those nights when he thought he heard the intruder, my father always came to my room first. I think it never occurred to him that someone might steal Darlene or Celia or Baby; my absence was the only one that he could truly imagine, the only absence that would leave the family somehow intact.

Sometimes he would rest his hand on my head and say, "Go back to sleep, Gracie. Everything's fine." But I could never sleep after that. I would lie awake listening to my father's robe swishing in the hallway, willing him to go back to bed. I was waiting for this mysterious man who needed so desperately to get to me. I imagined he wore dashing armor and carried a sword in a silver sheath. I wished he would hurry up.

Fifth Grade:

A Criminal

History

*I*t happened in a falling-down stable behind the train tracks in the season of the snow, in a place where it never snowed except that year, so that when you say "the season of the snow" everyone knows you are talking about 1978. In the minds of many, the whole event has been chalked up to the snowiness.

Looking back, I can see that Miss Saint John was already a changed woman long before we knew about her and Rodney. In October, the color of her lipstick went from light coral to burgundy. In November, during the Thanksgiving break, she dyed her hair red. Her dresses got tighter, her heels higher, her fingernails longer. She was transforming before our very eyes into a woman rather than the person we had always known. Before she dyed her hair, I had always simply thought of her as our teacher, and I imagine the other kids felt the same. It never occurred to me to wonder what kind of house she went home to in the evenings, or whom she ate dinner with. She was always there when I got to school in the morning and she was there when I left. It was as if the school itself had given birth to Miss Saint John.

At some point, though, she began showing up late to class. We'd all be sitting in our desks after the first bell had rung, and her chair at the front of the room would be vacant. The box on the chalkboard where she wrote each night's homework assignment would be empty as well. She'd show up halfway through the pledge of allegiance and spill her papers on the desk, turn and salute the flag just in time to mutter the final words . . . indivisible, with liberty and justice for all.

She began to look older, too, like a woman who never slept, with dark circles under her eyes. She'd sip coffee throughout the day and nap during recess, when Doris, the big, aggressive girl from the teacher's college, would take us out to the field behind the school and make us engage in something she called "organized play"— competitive sports such as War and Revenge that pitted the entire class against one student and resulted in total humiliation for the chosen one.

I'VE NEVER BEEN very good at remembering numbers. I remember his, though, because that's how we addressed his letters: Rodney Rouse, 84368 ASH-2, LA State Prison, Angola, Louisiana. During those four months, October to January, we wrote him every week. Each of us at our own desk on Fridays after recess, carefully practicing the cursive we'd been taught by Miss Saint John. We asked him how many brothers he had, how many sisters, if he had a dog and if so where did he keep it. We told him about our own dogs, their charming ways, and about neighbor boys who worked on their cars in the driveway. Those neighbors with their blaring radios and sultry girlfriends, their cans of beer propped on the hood, were the closest most of us had ever come to the criminal element.

Our letter-writing sessions gradually became longer. In the begin-

FIFTH GRADE: A CRIMINAL HISTORY

ning we spent half an hour after recess each Friday writing to Rodney, but eventually we wrote to him for forty-five minutes at a time, then an hour. One Friday the final bell rang and I realized we had been writing to Rodney since lunch. We often ran out of paper and had to borrow it from Miss Saint John. Naturally, we ran out of things to say as well. Everyone would be asking for the bathroom pass or the water pass, inventing reasons to go to the storage closet and retrieve important items from their backpacks, just to pass the time. In the beginning Miss Saint John wrote to Rodney on pieces of notebook paper, same as us, but eventually she began bringing fancy stationery to class, thin sheets of paper in soft shades of pink and yellow, envelopes with edges cut to look like lace. If you had a question to ask while she was writing to Rodney, you could forget it.

"Not now," she would snap. "Go back to your seat." It was shocking to see her behave that way, Miss Saint John to whom we had sworn our hearts. Most of the boys wanted to marry her and most of the girls wanted to be her—with her long hair and prairie skirts, her perpetually tanned skin and her bolo tie that fastened with a turquoise stone. I felt, some days, as if she had abandoned us. Angel felt it too. So did Michael Elder, and Sheila Mars, and Boyd Suskind, and Cindy Grimes, and Bobby Busby.

We became accustomed to Miss Saint John's late arrivals, but we knew she never missed one nation, under God, indivisible, with liberty and justice for all. The last Monday in January, hands started clapping patriotically over hearts when the last line of the pledge approached. To our dismay Miss Saint John did not show up. A couple of minutes after the pledge was over and we had slumped into our seats, Michael Elder went to the board and said, "What's he done? What's old Rodney done?"

"I bet he stole a car," Billy Rossbottom volunteered. Michael Elder wrote *steeling* on the board.

"I think he killed somebody," said Kathy Bluett. *Murder*, Michael wrote.

Angel, who watched a lot of pirate movies, accused him of marauding. And so on, until the list snaked all the way across the bottom of the blackboard. Then Michael drew a person who was supposed to be Rodney sitting in a chair. He drew sparks flying out of Rodney's eyes and mouth and fingers, fire shooting from the top of his head. He dropped the chalk into the holder, scraped his fingernails across the board, and marched back to his seat.

I can still see Boyd Suskind clearly, turning in his seat to extract his big legs from under his desk, standing up slowly, and walking to the front of the room. His pants were a little too short, and you could see that one of his white socks was new and one of them was old, because one gleamed like a Tide commercial and one was dingy brown. He picked up a piece of chalk and wrote on the board with agonizing slowness and in impeccable cursive, *Malicious intent to steal Miss Saint John*. At that moment, the big, smart boy who ate ketchup and mayonnaise sandwiches for lunch, and who had until that point remained largely anonymous, gained stature among us. The fact that Boyd had applied his sometimes off-putting intellect to the task of insulting Rodney made us see him in a different light.

We were sitting in our desks, trying unsuccessfully to sound out the words, when Boyd pronounced them for us: "Malicious intent. It means he's got an idea in his head, and the idea is a bad one, and he knows it will cause her harm." Boyd was proselytizing in front of the board like that, the chalk poised in his left hand, when Miss Saint John walked in. They say what separates humans from monkeys is an opposable thumb, but I think, instead, it is the ability to look back on one defining event in our lives and recognize it as the one that ruined us. I have often thought of that moment as the moment that changed Rodney's fate.

Miss Saint John stood at the back of the classroom and looked at the board, silently reading the list of offenses. Boyd, thinking perhaps that he could slip back into the anonymity he had always enjoyed, began to move slowly toward his seat; as he did so Michael's

FIFTH GRADE: A CRIMINAL HISTORY

drawing of Rodney in the electric chair came into view. Miss Saint John walked to the front of the room, grabbed Boyd by the arm, and said, "Get out of my classroom. I can't stand to look at your face."

Boyd stared at her blankly for a moment. You could tell there was something he wanted to say, but he didn't say it. Michael Elder, of course, did not confess that it was he who had started the whole thing, and not one of us stood up for Boyd. Miss Saint John was squeezing his arm so hard that her knuckles turned white. When at last she released him, there were little half-moons in the flesh above his elbow, and one of her fingernails had even broken the skin. As Boyd lumbered out of the room, defeated and ashamed, I realized that what he had wanted to tell her was not the truth about the chalkboard game. What I believe he meant to tell her, what he may have told her if the rest of us had not been sitting there, was that he loved her. It was obvious that he did. The rest of us cherished and envied her. But what Boyd felt, I believe, went beyond our fifth grade emotions. That was why he stayed after school to wash the chalk-boards, why he volunteered for bathroom monitor even though it made the other boys dislike him, why he accompanied his mother to every PTA meeting, dressed in a dark gray suit and tie, looking like a man. There had always been something adult about him, as if he had a grown-up mind trapped inside a kid's body, or, more accurately, an adult mind and body trapped inside a childish age. He shouldn't have been eleven years old. Like the smart kids who skip a grade or two of school, he should have skipped the years themselves, so that he could have moved about in the world as an adult rather than as a child.

Boyd was absent for the rest of the week. There were rumors that he had been expelled or had run away, or that he was literally dying of lovesickness, or that he was hitchhiking all the way to Angola State Prison to get even with Rodney. The following Monday he showed up, looking thin and pale, as if he hadn't eaten for days. We all gathered around his desk that morning before Miss Saint John arrived, asking questions he refused to answer, and at lunch we fought over the seat next to him in the cafeteria. Angel gave him half of her peanut-butter sandwich, and I was lucky enough to squeeze into the seat straight across from him and share my powdered doughnuts. Angel and I were ready to do anything for Boyd. Once a week in chapel we were required to recite the Ten Commandments, the first being, "Take no other gods before me." This collective idolatry felt vaguely pagan and punishable, and therefore all the more exciting.

After recess on the day Boyd returned, Miss Saint John said she had something to tell us. She said that if we really cared about her—"about me as a person," she said—we would be happy for her. She said that, first and foremost, we had to understand that people do things they're sorry for, and then, if they ask God's forgiveness they can be cleansed, made new in the eyes of the Lord. She said that if God can forget something we should be able to forget it too. She said that if a man does something criminal—such as forging a great number of checks in amounts totaling over one hundred thousand dollars—and then that man spends time in jail where he is able to contemplate his actions and where he realizes the error of his ways, he can and should be accepted back into society. She opened her arms when she said this, an unusually dramatic gesture for a usually untheatrical woman. Her blue knit top stretched across her breasts. She said, "I have spent a great deal of time with Rodney Rouse over the last few months. You may or may not be aware that I have made several trips to Angola to see him."

At this there was an audible shifting in chairs, a collective intake of breath. Michael Elder shouted, "No way!" Kim Stafford said, "Yup," under her breath, as if she had suspected it all along. Marla Dufresne started sobbing, and Miss Saint John said, "Is there a problem, Marla?" and Marla said, "No ma'am, may I be excused please I'm having a stomach ache."

We all looked at Boyd for direction. He just sat there with his arms folded across his chest, staring at the floor.

"Good. As I was saying, I have seen Rodney on several occasions. I have had the chance to get to know him, not as a prisoner but as a person, a child of God, and I do not mind saying, as a man." Angel gave me a knowing look. *As a man.* What was that supposed to mean? It sounded suspicious and vulgar. It would certainly explain her short skirts and long nails, her red hair, maybe it even had something to do with the dark circles under her eyes.

"Rodney has been granted early parole for good behavior. He was an exemplary prisoner. Your letters reminded him of what the real world is like, the world where normal people do normal things every day and don't get caught because they're not doing anything to get caught for. They just treat one another with respect and the consequences are beautiful. You should be proud of yourselves."

I was not feeling proud, but stupid, as if those early letters I wrote about Matthew Fips washing the car out in the driveway with his big blonde girlfriend Besty Paducah, who brought him vanilla milkshakes and french fries from the Rally's drive-through and wore cowboy boots with her short-shorts, were now being used against me. I also felt as if I had committed some sort of felony, even though I wasn't sure what that meant. I had the vague feeling that we were all felons and it was Miss Saint John's fault.

"Rodney is coming to Mobile. He's taking the Saturday bus. He asked me to marry him and I said yes."

Angel fell out of her chair. We heard a loud crash and there she was on the floor, legs sprawled, humming the theme song to *The Love Boat.* She always hummed when she did something extraordinarily clumsy; it was her trademark.

"Grace, please help Angel," Miss Saint John said, not missing a beat. "Now don't worry. Nothing is going to change. We still have almost four months together and I will be the same teacher you have known all along, only now I will be Mrs. Rouse instead of Miss Saint John, and I'll be taking a week off to honeymoon in Gatlinburg, Tennessee."

All that day Boyd was silent. Every time Miss Saint John asked him a question, acting as if no bad blood had passed between them, as if she had not sent him to the principal's office or broken his heart, Boyd just said, "I don't know," even though we all knew he did, and then she went on to someone else, but we all pretended not to know, in silent protest and in honor of Boyd. On Tuesday he was quiet again, and secretive, speaking to no one. That night a cold front moved in from Mississippi and the temperature dropped to forty-five. On Wednesday we gathered around Boyd during recess, following our weekly round of War, a game in which two countries face off across a border and you are required to slam your classmates with a hard rubber ball, or cannon, until they are declared dead. If you hit them too hard you are removed from the battle by the War Crimes Tribunal, which was really just Doris from the teacher's college. We were all a bit bruised and battered from the game, and freezing, now that the thermometer outside the Sippee Shack read thirty-nine—but refreshed by Boyd's pronouncement under the Love Tree on the south side of the playground: "I have a plan. You will be made aware of it when the time comes." It sounded alluringly prophetic, and on the bus home I closed my eyes and fantasized about him, Boyd as John the Baptist, ranting in the wilderness, the crazy man, chosen of God, who knew the truth and proclaimed it. On Thursday he began organizing. I was certain that something big was going to happen, because we could see our breath in front of our faces, an unbelievable magic in a place where we usually wore short sleeves on Christmas Day.

By Friday we all knew our parts. Boyd explained The Plan beneath the domed jungle gym on the playground. We shivered in our light jackets, all except Danny Frank who had moved here from Wisconsin and was therefore prepared for the cold in a thick down jacket and gloves. Angel and I were to bring flowers. Danny was to snag handcuffs from the duffel bag his dad carried every morning when he went to work at the FBI. Tracy Johnson, a mean skinny redhead whose mother was a substitute teacher, had to bring the music. The Plan was to scare Rodney into leaving Miss Saint John alone; just how we were going to accomplish that remained Boyd's secret.

That night Angel came to my house for a sleepover, and we made carnations out of colored tissue paper in front of the television. The weatherman interrupted *Little House on the Prairie* to say that the temperature had dropped to twenty-nine and there was a slight chance of precipitation. Angel was so startled she sliced her hand open with the scissors, and my mother bandaged the wound while Angel hummed "Closer My God to Thee."

At ten o'clock Saturday morning we gathered at Dreamland Skating Rink, made more brazen by the snow, which had begun to fall during the night and formed a white veil on the ground. Across the street loomed Bay View Baptist Church, its white steeple pointing heavenward, the gold cross edged with snow. Many of the kids had never seen snow before, so there was a great deal of excitement. The boys were acting more aggressive than usual, punching one another in the arms, wrestling, playing thumb war. After the last parent drove away we left the warmth of the rink and marched down the street to the Greyhound station.

The bus from Angola was scheduled to arrive at 10:39 A.M. At 10:30, Miss Saint John's brand new Chevy pulled into the parking lot. As she swung her legs around and climbed out, her black skirt rode up over her thighs. She was wearing garters, which I had never seen before on a real live woman, just in the dirty pictures Mamie Harris stole from her brother's glove box. Her hair, which was usually tied up in a ponytail or French twist, fell in soft waves down her back. She looked beautiful but a little silly in her short skirt and heels, with the snow swirling all around her. She shut the door of the Chevy and walked over to us, her heels sinking into the powder.

"Enjoying the snow?" she asked nervously, and everyone agreed that yes, the snow was wonderful, and she said we ought to gather a little bit of it in our hands and take it home and put it in our freezers, just so we could remember. Then she went right up to Boyd—they were eye level with one another, and so close that the frost of their breath met and mingled between them—and she said, "Okay, Mr. Suskind, what is this all about?"

Boyd looked down at his feet, then up the street to Dreamland's droopy sign, then back at us. Finally he met Miss Saint John's eyes straight on. "I came to apologize. I feel bad about that incident at the blackboard, and we all wanted to come and welcome Rodney to town. We've talked about it and we just want you to be happy."

For a moment she looked skeptical, and then she broke into a wide grin and wrapped her arms around Boyd's neck and pulled him toward her. The hug lasted a long time. Most of the boys in the class would have sacrificed their ten-speeds to be wrapped up in Miss Saint John's long arms like that, her hair spilling over their shoulders and catching on their scarves, her breasts pressed up against them. When Boyd stepped back, he had a smear of lipstick on his cheek where her mouth had brushed against him. Seeing them like that, I thought that they could be a couple, that they looked good together and given a few years it might work out for them, they might have a baby and take vacations to Six Flags Over Georgia.

"We've made something for you," Boyd said.

"That's sweet! What is it?"

"It's a secret. It's down at the stable behind the old train tracks. We were hoping we could take you and Rodney there."

"Well." She put her hands in the pockets of her suede jacket and prodded the snow with her heel. I was almost glad to hear the doubt in Miss Saint John's voice; part of me was hoping that she would flat-out refuse, but she looked at us, perhaps believing that her entire fifth grade class would not lie to her. "Is it true?"

"Yes," we all chimed in. When I look back, I always hear my own voice as the weakest among them. I always tell myself that my "yes" was little more than a whisper, and that she should have known from the quietness of it that there was something wrong.

"We made something for you," Sheila Mars said, and looked relieved once she had said it. That was her line. She had pulled it off.

"It took hours," Bobby Busby added.

There was a great deal of head-nodding and encouragement, until finally Miss Saint John said, "All right. I'm glad you changed your minds. You're really going to like him."

The bus arrived ten minutes late and Rodney was the last one out of it, a tall, good-looking man in a tweed coat and khakis. He didn't look at all like someone who had just gotten out of prison. His brown hair was very short and neat, and the thing that most startled me about him was that he had deep dimples that made him look like Magnum, P.I. I'm not sure what I had expected—that he would be dirty and wearing a striped uniform like you see in the movies, I guess, that he'd be missing half his teeth and would come bounding out of the bus with guns a'blazing. As soon as he stepped off the bus Miss Saint John rushed into his arms, and he was kissing her all over her hair and neck, her face and arms and hands, like he couldn't get enough of her. He had his hand on her behind and her skirt rose up on the back of her legs so that I could see the garters again. There were little red bows where the straps met the stockings, and a broken vein twisted like a tiny blue river high on her right leg. We were all hanging back a little, behind Boyd, and after they had finished kissing, Miss Saint John took Rodney by the hand and led him over to us.

"Kids, this is Rodney Rouse, my fiancé. Rodney, these are my fifth graders."

He nodded and gave us a little wave, then said he wanted to thank us for our letters, which had helped him to pass the time in a most satisfactory way, and above all he wanted to thank us for helping him get to know this wonderful woman, Deborah. A little whisper went through the crowd. We had never known her first name. The name made her seem more vulnerable somehow, more like one of us. Boyd reached out and shook Rodney's hand, introducing himself, then he went through the entire group, announcing each of our names. When Miss Saint John asked Rodney if he would mind walking the quarter-mile with us to the stable, Rodney said, "Are you kidding? You can take me anywhere."

Boyd walked in front with Rodney and Miss Saint John, chatting them up about the weather and politics, the recent presidential election. Boyd seemed like a regular grown-up, a man far above and beyond us, going on about Jimmy Carter as if he knew the man personally. The rest of us traipsed along behind, the snow soaking our ankles, and I began to wonder if Boyd no longer wanted to mess with Rodney at all, they seemed to be getting along so well.

Finally we came to the end of the dirt road and crossed over the tracks. Moments later the deserted stable came into view, partially hidden behind a row of pine trees whose limbs bowed slightly under the weight of the snow. "It's in here," Boyd said. We all crowded in behind him. Even though the stable hadn't been used in years, there was a slight, pleasant odor of horse manure. Most of the stall doors were missing, and the dirt floor was littered with hay. Boyd had strung white crepe paper from one stall to the next to form a sort of aisle down the middle of the stable, and at the far end of the aisle stood a small wooden table, on top of which was a black Bible and a bunch of chrysanthemums in a Folgers can.

"What is all this?" Miss Saint John asked. Rodney had an arm around her shoulder. She looked very small beside him.

"Since you're getting married in Bayou la Battre and none of us can be there, I thought we'd have our own wedding ceremony right here," Boyd said.

"I don't know," Miss Saint John said, but Rodney was being good-natured about the whole thing. He clapped Boyd on the shoulder like a good son. "Why not? I've been dying to make it official for months."

"Okay," Boyd said, before Miss Saint John could protest again.

"The bride has to go outside while we prepare the groom. Mary Fay, you're the flower girl. When you hear the bridal march, you come in first." He looked at me and Angel and said, "You're the bridesmaids, so you come in after Miss Saint John. Did you bring the flowers?" We pulled the six paper carnations out of the Delchamps bag and handed them to Miss Saint John. I felt relieved to discover that all I had to do was be a bridesmaid in a pretend wedding. I didn't see how any harm could come from that.

"Bobby and Jeremy are the groomsmen, so you're going to stand up here with old Rodney. Michael's got the honor of giving the bride away. Everybody else can just have a seat along the sides."

Mary Fay, Angel, Michael, and I went outside with Miss Saint John. She wanted to know what we thought of Rodney, and we said he seemed very nice, handsome too. After a couple of minutes we heard the bridal march playing loudly on the boom box, so Mary Fay opened the door of the stable and walked down the aisle very slowly, tossing dried potpourri as she went, aiming at people's heads. Miss Saint John followed, arm in arm with Michael, then Angel, then me. Rodney was wearing a black top-hat and cummerbund, and Boyd stood behind the makeshift pulpit, Bible in hand, wearing a clergy collar made of black and white construction paper. Miss Saint John let go of Michael's arm at the front, and Tracy cut the music.

"We are gathered here today to join our lovely teacher, Miss Saint John, with this convict," Boyd began.

"Boyd!" Miss Saint John looked like she might slap him or something.

Rodney laughed but his teeth were closed, and I couldn't tell if it was a real laugh or a fake one. "It's all right, hon. Just a little joke. Right, Boyd?"

"Sorry, no hard feelings," Boyd said.

Rodney reached out and touched Miss Saint John on the shoulder, and she seemed okay again, calmed.

"Now, Miss Saint John, repeat after me. I, Deborah Saint John,"

"I, Deborah Saint John,"

"Do take this prisoner, Rodney Rouse—"

"That's enough from you, Mr. Suskind," Miss Saint John said. She grabbed Rodney's hand and turned to leave.

"Stay put," Boyd said, reaching into his jacket and pulling out a gun. At first I thought it was a toy, it must be a toy, but I could tell from the way Rodney responded, backing away slowly, his arms spread at his sides in a gesture of surrender, that it was real.

"Whoa, now, son, let's not allow this thing to get out of hand."

Miss Saint John must have still believed she had some power over Boyd, that he still viewed her as his teacher and superior, because instead of backing away she rushed toward him. "This isn't funny. Give that to me." She reached for the gun and he held her off with his free hand, and when she kept coming at him he fired a shot into the air that brought a storm of wood chips down on our heads. A couple of people jumped up like they were going to leave, but Boyd said, "Stay in your places, everybody. Miss Saint John wanted to have a wedding so we're going to have a wedding."

"Look, man." Jeremy was moving toward him slowly, his soft, high voice echoing in the startled silence. "Let's forget about this. Let's all go on home."

Boyd looked at Jeremy and said, "You think I won't use this? Now let's just do this thing. You two face each other, let's get you married."

"And then you'll let us go?" Rodney sounded more exhausted than surprised, and not at all afraid. Maybe he didn't believe that Boyd had it in him to do any harm. "I'm asking for your word, son. That will be the end of it?"

Boyd nodded. "A simple ceremony. Then everyone goes home."

If you closed your eyes and listened to just the cadence of the words rather than the words themselves, it was almost like a real wedding. That's what I did, just to get through it, to keep myself from thinking about how embarrassed Miss Saint John must be, having to say those things.

"I, Deborah Saint John, do take this prisoner, Rodney Rouse, to be my criminal husband, to fear and to loathe, in anger and in sadness, in ugly lust and ignorance, from this day forward, 'til death do us part."

"Louder," Boyd said whenever her voice started to falter, and he would make her start over again. This happened several times. Then it was Rodney's turn.

"I, Rodney Rouse, do take this woman, Deborah Saint John, to be the wife I don't deserve, because I have conned her the way I conned others before her, and I have tricked her into marrying me, and our union shall be shameful in the eyes of the Lord, from this day forward, 'til death do us part." Rodney's face was turning red, and he was sweating despite the cold. I felt sorry for him.

"The ring," Boyd said.

Danny was standing a couple of feet from the bride and groom, looking at the ground. "I don't want to," he said.

"It's too late to back out now," Boyd said.

"But I wouldn't have brought them if I knew."

Boyd made a little clicking sound with the gun, the way they do in movies, and Danny took a pair of handcuffs out of his jacket pocket. He put one cuff around Miss Saint John's right wrist, and the other around Rodney's left.

"I now declare you criminal and wife," Boyd said. "You may kiss the bride."

Miss Saint John was sobbing now. When Rodney pulled her toward him tenderly, she wouldn't meet his eyes. She just rested her head on his chest.

"Kiss her," Boyd demanded.

"Sweetheart," Rodney said, lifting her chin with his free hand. He kissed her very softly on the lips and said, "It's over, okay? It's nothing. It's going to be fine."

Boyd had his arms folded across his chest. Standing there with that snowy light shining down on him, he looked even taller than usual. "That's no kiss."

"Look, son. Can't you see you've upset her." I could tell Rodney was getting mad. "That's enough, now."

"You're not getting out of here until you do it right. Kiss her the way you do when you fuck her, Rodney."

It must have been instinct, a momentary lapse in logic brought on by fury, that made Rodney lunge toward Boyd, forgetting the handcuffs that joined him and Miss Saint John. Boyd unfolded his arms and fired. Later he would insist it was an accident. He would hold fast to his statement that the safety was off, it wasn't his intention, he only wanted to scare the man. The two of them went down, Rodney and Miss Saint John, and there was a shocked moment during which we didn't know who had been hit. Then Miss Saint John was screaming, and we knew it was Rodney, and Boyd said, "Somebody go get help," and that's when the spell broke and we were released from him. We all ran out the stable and up the dirt road, slipping in the snow as we went, and crying. No one stayed behind with Miss Saint John.

We all had to go to the police station. They interviewed each of us separately. It was on the television in the waiting room that we learned the bullet had lodged in Rodney's spine; he was paralyzed from the waist down and was not expected to walk again. We were the lead story on every local station. We even made the national news with Dan Rather. The reporters interviewed other teachers at the school, only one of whom admitted knowing that Miss Saint John was engaged to an ex-convict. For weeks after that, the phone at my house rang constantly, as it did at every other house where one of Miss Saint John's fifth grade students lived. Every few years a kid will pull out a gun in some small-town school in Mississippi or Kentucky or Arkansas, or an anniversary of the fake wedding will roll around, and the interest in us will resurface. The local newspapers and tele-

FIFTH GRADE: A CRIMINAL HISTORY

vision stations will decide to do a "Where are they now?" and we all have to take our phones off the hook until the story gets cold.

I may go for days or weeks without thinking of the thing we did, but there is always this town and I live in it. Bobby Busby manages the Bank of Mobile, and occasionally I stop in to see him. I sit across the big oak desk from him, and we talk about my recent move back home from New York City, or about the new bakery on Government Boulevard, or about the latest game between Auburn and the Crimson Tide. Whenever I need a new dress I go to Cindy Grimes's shop at Hillcrest Plaza, and I buy all my groceries at the small store run by Sheila Mars, even though it's the most expensive in town. Those days when I need to sit in the dark and drink I go to Haley's on Cottage Hill, where Michael Elder is a bartender. He's never been married and over the years he has dated half the girls in our class, including Angel.

Boyd spent two years at a juvenile detention center and when he got out he was withdrawn again, and quiet. He got a two-year degree from Bishop State Junior College and became a Century 21 man, and during a brief run of self-confidence and good luck, his face reigned over the intersection of Government Boulevard and Cody Road across the bay in Fairhope, plastered across a billboard under the heading, "Southeast Region Agent of the Month."

Rodney took disability and got fat, and every now and then I'll see him being wheeled down Cottage Hill by his second wife, an aerobics teacher named Sarah. Miss Saint John quit teaching immediately after the incident in the stable. She took a job as a receptionist at a dentist's office, then moved away in 1985 after the divorce, looking much older than her thirty-three years. Sometimes I wonder if their love just couldn't handle the thing we did to them, if she could not endure being both his lover and his nurse, hauling him into the bed and pulling off his pants so that she could sit astride him, moving for the both of them, while his useless legs just lay there. I know *that* part of him still worked, because he and Sarah have a nine-year-old son. Every now and then I'll see the kid in a neighbor's yard, and I swear he looks at me as if he knows who I am and what I did.

The last time I saw Deborah Saint John was 1984. She was standing in front of the Delchamps on Schillinger Road, holding a bag of groceries, waiting for the bus. I said hello to her and she smiled politely, but she didn't seem to recognize me. We haven't had another snowfall since 1978.

FIFTH GRADE: A CRIMINAL HISTORY

Monkey

Stew

*M*y mother does not like to hear my father's stories of the war. She was alone in San Francisco at the time, awaiting his return, pacing back and forth on the thin blue carpet of their small apartment. The draft had sent him west to serve the Navy on a boat called the *Enterprise*. "It's the size of five football fields," she says. "Five. That's enormous. I don't see how it floats."

I've seen pictures of my mother in that Richmond district studio, stretched out like some starlet on a bed that folded out of the wall. Back then she wore white lipstick and dresses up to here. Finally she got tired of waiting. She packed her suitcase and turned in her key and drove all the way home to Alabama. She made an adventure of it, stopping at every roadside attraction along the way. Among her discoveries were Sang Froid, a grizzly bear who could play the piano; Jada Sweet, America's thinnest woman; a silent movie titled *The Dudes and Darlings of West Texas*; and a three-day revival where she allowed herself to be saved by a bald man in a crumpled suit, even though the truth was she'd already been saved at the tender age of twelve.

During that trip my mother ate tater tots at roadside diners and took photographs of dead animals on the highway—"two things I had never done before and would never do again," she says—as if, on that trip, she was possessed by the spirit of some other, less sensible woman. She kept a list of the names of all the remote and slumbering towns she drove through: Bakersfield, Red Branch, Pleasant Hollow, Fellows Way. By the time she got to Alabama she was certain that marriage was not for her, that she was destined to become a traveler instead. Those two weeks in Alabama she slept in her old bedroom of her parents' house, as if she had never left. She dreamt of streamlined silver campers that would carry her coast to coast, and she bought dozens of rolls of film to prepare for the many strange and wonderful things she would surely see.

Eventually she went back to San Francisco, but only after having a good long talk with my grandmother. My grandmother made a big pot of coffee, put an Elvis record on the turntable and said, "He's your husband. You can't just up and leave."

Once when the *Enterprise* was in port for the weekend, my father jumped off a cable car because he thought he saw my mother walking down the street. The woman he saw had dark hair and was wearing a summer dress. He ran down the streets of San Francisco, a Navy man in white cap and skivvies, looking like a lunatic, calling out her name. He never caught up with her. To this day he swears the woman was my mother.

"I would have known her anywhere," he says. "The hair, the dress, how she turned on her tall yellow heel. She was at the fruit stand when I saw her, examining tangerines."

"It was an illusion," my mother says. "Your father has been known to have them. He couldn't possibly have seen me because I was right here in Alabama at the time. I could not conceivably have been at a fruit stand, looking at tangerines and wearing a pair of tall yellow heels."

Years later, when I am grown and single, having hightailed it out of New York City and embarked on my own marathon home to Alabama, my mother tells me in confidence that it was indeed she who stood at the fruit stand that day in San Francisco. She says that even true love has its doubts. She says she was doubting my father then, wondering what she'd gotten herself into. She says there was a period of three months while he was away that she didn't wear her wedding band. She says that when she walked away, she thought she was walking away for good.

When I ask why she came back to him, she says, "Love don't come easy, you gotta get it where you can," but I think she was just quoting an old country song.

Sometimes I can see her, thirty years younger, turning on her tall yellow heels to leave. My father chases after; he wants to tell her what he has seen. He wants to tell her about monkey stew in Thailand, and how he didn't mean to eat it, how it was served to him over a bed of rice just like pork or beef or chicken. Mostly he would like to tell her that he dreams of her each night, that he paces from bow to stern on the deck of the *Enterprise* mumbling her name.

The Girl

in the

Fall-Away

Dress

I am cruising down Market Street when I see her. I have been driving distractedly, glancing out the side window to the view of San Francisco laid out beneath me, the white layers of fog parting over the Bay. The city is new to me, it is the place I have always dreamed of, and when I arrived here last week via Highway 1, thinking what that meant—that this was the first highway, the alpha of all highways, the beginning of a system of traversing and leaving and arriving thought up by FDR decades ago—it was like coming for the first time upon some foreign place that I had seen in my memory for years, a place to which I had never been but which had always appeared more vividly in my mind than the town where I grew up. Now, looking out at the Bay Bridge stretched over the gray water, I am wondering how it is that I have lived my entire life without driving this winding street through this perfect stretch of city.

I have just overtaken the hill when I see them. At the top of

Market, a walkway gently arches over the street. This walkway, too, is a figment of my imagination; that is, the walkway was imagined by me long before I ever saw the real thing, so that when I did see it, four days ago, I averted my eyes from the traffic and stared in ecstatic awe at the thing I had thought up, that had been thought up likewise by someone else, or by a committee of someone elses whom I never knew, who nevertheless had my exact-same vision.

I haven't been up on the walkway yet, have only viewed it from my car, because I am afraid that if I go up there and observe the walkway from a different perspective it will become not the thing I thought of, but something else entirely. So I drive up and down Market Street fifteen or so times a day, but not once have I seen anyone walking across the suspended path. Thus, it has occurred to me that the path is not there at all, but continues to be the figment I always believed it to be, so that if I pulled into one of the driveways crouched beneath the tall houses crowded onto the hill, and took the spiraling path that leads up to the walkway, and placed a foot upon the cement, the whole illusion would give way beneath me and I would fall to the street below, making an unfortunate and bloody ruckus. I drive back and forth hoping for some sign that I have not made this bridge up, waiting to see an actual body walking across it, or a bicyclist bicycling, or a runner running, or an escapee escaping. *Someone.*

Today there are two. Two girls, one dressed in black, one in white, one thin and one not so thin, one blonde and one brunette, each holding a broom with both hands. The girls face one another, their feet wide apart, knees bent, shoulders thrust forward. Their dresses are long and flowing and seem to be made of silk, and they have no sleeves or straps, but are wrapped around the girls' bodies sarong-style, so that they move the way wind might move, waltzlike and impromptu. The thin blonde in the black dress swings her broom at the plumpish brunette in the white dress, brings it up to her cheek in slow motion, and the girl in the white dress responds likewise, moving her face away from the broom, lifting one leg high and turning in a complete circle, and bringing her own broom down against the legs of her opponent, who turns now and lifts her broom again.

I have slowed to watch the girls, living proof of the reality of my walkway. The other drivers seem not to have noticed this demonstration, or not to care, speeding past in complete indifference. Approaching the underlip of the bridge and fearful of losing sight of the girls, I ease down on the brake. Someone behind me begins honking just as the plump girl raises her arms, hefting the broom high above her.

There is a sense of unloosening, I feel it in my gut even before the dress that moves like wind has fallen away. It is as though I am standing inches from the girl and can see the knot slipping just above her soft breasts, the silk sliding over her chest, her thighs, the whiteness of her skin and the thick lovely folds of her bottom and the twin dimples above the place where her cheeks press outward from her back revealed as the dress moves up and outward. The dress is suspended somewhere above the girl, just out of reach, for a long moment before it floats downward, falling away from her, over the edge of the walkway, descending to meet my windshield, passing over the glass in a quick caress before a corner of it catches on the side mirror. I take the white silk in my hands and pull the fallen dress into the car.

Having passed beneath the walkway I look in my rearview mirror and see her, the naked, dark-haired girl, shaven clean, all fresh and pink in the wind, her breasts upright and round. The broom stands at her side, bristles up; her fingers curl around the handle in an absurd mockery of *An American Gothic*. The girl looks stunned and accusatory, as if she might leap over the bridge and confront me, the driver with out-of-state plates descending the hill with her dress. She drops the broom and crosses one hand over her breasts, cups the other between her legs, then turns toward her companion as I round the curve, one hand plunged into the soft mound of silk.

THE GIRL IN THE FALL-AWAY DRESS

It occurs to me that this is the kind of story Ivan would tell. *Gracie,* he would say, looking me straight in the eyes. *I saw this girl on the bridge today. Her dress fell off of her, just like that.* He would say it with such conviction, but he would have no evidence, and I would take his story to be make-believe. Somewhere in this city, Ivan is spinning stories for someone else.

HER

The wind has hands that take me up. Out there the Bay shimmers, the water pushes the cool hands toward me. Down below the cars move, the buses screech to top the hill, the workers come home, the drivers watch. Up here it is the two of us. She wears only black, even in summer, the city's coldest season. I wear only white. We are a simple entity, two halves. Up here on the bridge, or down there in our tiny house that we inherited from our father, our house with its high narrow windows, here or there we are in opposition.

She challenged me to this duel, a game having only two rules: we must move at a fraction of our normal speed, so as to bring on exhaustion more quickly, and the one who stops first loses. The one who loses leaves. To the victor goes the house, the turquoise carpet from Turkey, the yellowing walls of the bedrooms, the old gas stove, the pointy roof. It is too late for us to live together. I have chosen a man she despises. She has chosen no one, or rather, she has chosen me. She believes she is my mother, my teacher, my cook, my one-who-knows-best. Five years since our father died, and she has named herself my guardian, though I am nineteen and do not need to be guarded.

I am certain of my victory, for I am the strongest. She eats only vegetables and grainy things, stringy plants that grow in a window box above the kitchen sink. Her legs beneath the black sarong are thin. Her arms become tired while vacuuming. She has not made love to anyone in years, and I believe, though she protests, that she is too weak for passion. Only days ago she came upon me in the living room, sitting on the couch, my hands propped on the shoulders of the man whom she despises.

"No more," she said, seeing his head plunged between my thighs, my fingers tracing the path of moles on his shoulders as I sat up, hips thrust over the edge of the cushions, loving the image of him bowed before me. "Not in this house."

"The house belongs to both of you," he said, propping his chin on my thigh to take up my side. A practical man. A man not unlike my sister, possessed by an argumentative disposition.

That night, after he had left and we had fought until our throats were sore from shouting, she proposed the duel. I wondered aloud whether it wasn't overly dramatic.

"Then come up with something better," she said—the same words, I thought, that *he* would have chosen.

At first I am ashamed to be standing here on the walkway, the silk clinging to my thighs, to my stomach that will not shrink, to my body that is too big. For years I tried to make myself smaller, until I met him, the man who said, "I love your size," pressing his hands deep into the skin of my back, resting his cheek against my inner thigh.

The straws of the broom brush my face, a cue that it is my turn to move, to lift my leg and turn and come back around to her. The dance proceeds. We have been up here for an hour at least. I am becoming tired, but I am determined to outlast her. Then there is the gust of wind, the lifting, the quick parting of silk from skin. I see the dress suspended above me, airborne, and understand that I am naked, on display. I reach for the dress, but I am not quick enough.

A woman's hand reaches out of a window. I see a flash of red hair through the sunroof of a small silver car just before my dress disappears with the hand. Covering myself, I move toward my sister, thinking that she will come to my aid, that she will be the mother she has always been, that she will sacrifice her modesty for my own. I am waiting for her to unfold her dress, to wrap me up in it.

"I win," she says, then walks away, leaving me naked above the traffic. A chorus of honking starts up, and there are heads emerging from car windows, and children waving, and the chill of the fog on my skin. I crouch low to the sidewalk, my legs drawn up to my chest, my face buried in my knees. I try to make myself small, so small no one can see me. Soon my bones feel frozen.

Belly-down, I crawl toward the far end of the bridge, the opposite direction from our house, her house now, the house I lost to her. My lover's house is only a couple of hundred yards away, the purple house on the hill. I don't care if the wife is baking, the children watching television, the whole sweet family gathered round. He will have to take me in. The fog has drawn in close like a zipper. I make my way through the small squares of yard, the short driveways packed with cars, crouching behind fenders and blue garbage cans that have been set out for morning. Coming upon his purple house I go down on hands and knees, crawl around back like a cat come home for supper. There are lights in every room. Music drifts from the windows. I raise my head just above the sill. On the rectangular rug with green fringe around the edges, he is dancing with his wife. The children sit at the corners, clapping and singing, getting all the words wrong.

I tap the window screen. The whole family looks my way. The youngest boy, Sami, runs over and presses his nose against the screen. "She's naked!" he announces.

Tami, who is ten, asks, "Mother, is it wild?"

The six year old, Simon, whom his father considers clever, says, "I spy me a nudist. The nudist is at the window. She ain't wearing any clothes."

My lover's wife runs over and grabs the children. I say his name but he pretends not to hear me. "Call the police!" his wife says, as if I have not just said her husband's name, as if I am some stranger.

"No," I say to the wife, the children. "I've been here many times. There's a blue rug in Simon's bedroom. The toilet leaks when you flush it. The right rear burner is missing on the stove!" In this manner I attempt to validate myself, to assert my right to be here, but the wife is not listening. She is dragging the children upstairs, and they are screaming bloody murder. My lover stands in the hallway, holding the red rotary phone.

"There's a mad woman at my window," my lover says into the receiver. "She's not wearing any clothes."

DIAMOND

A naked woman on a bridge won't last long, not here or anywhere. At Mars Street, I turn and head back toward the bridge, planning to restore the dress to the girl. In the time it takes for me to negotiate San Francisco's serpentine roads and plentiful one-way streets, the girl has disappeared, and a yard sale has sprung up at the foot of the walkway.

A cardboard sign says, "Everything must go." A man slouches on the ground beside a small silver table with one broken leg. He is wearing an unusual sort of hat with a blue feather tucked into the band. The table is beautiful in an orphaned way; quite clearly it needs a home. The man is also selling a red feather boa, a snapping turtle in a yellow cage, an old sewing machine, a Speed Racer lunch box, a pair of army-issue binoculars, and a box of steno pads.

I park the car illegally in someone's driveway and leave it running. "How much is this table?" I ask the man, knocking my knuckles nonchalantly against the surface, as if the table barely interests me, as if I could take it or leave it.

"Why don't you take the steno pads instead?" he says. "I can let you have the whole box for fifty cents."

"No," I say. "I stopped for the table."

"This snapping turtle is seventeen years old," the man says, thrusting the cage in my direction. "Her name is Darren. She makes a fine pet. She eats very little and only needs to be walked twice a week. You can have her for seventy-five cents."

"I've never been good with turtles. How about the table?"

THE GIRL IN THE FALL-AWAY DRESS

"A feather boa has many uses. You can tie back your curtains with it, or create a comfortable bed for a pet, or wear it out on a special evening. This feather boa costs ninety cents, and that's my final offer."

I picture myself in the white dress that fell from the sky, the feather boa draped around my neck, presenting myself to Ivan with studied nonchalance. "I'll take it," I say. "The binoculars too. And the table?"

The man lets out a long, disappointed sigh. "What do you plan to do with it?" The blue feather in his unusual hat distracts me. I am unable to articulate.

"I just moved here," I say. "I'm going to put it in my kitchen."

"The table is five hundred dollars."

I tell him that his table is not made of gold. I tell him that his hat is ludicrous.

"Where do you come from?" he wants to know.

"Alabama."

He doesn't believe me. "What's the capital?" he demands.

"Montgomery."

"Okay," he says to the turtle. "She's an honest woman. Twenty dollars for the table. One-fifty for the feather boa and binoculars."

I pay him and put the goods in my trunk. He waves as I drive away, and I wave back, but then I realize that he is not looking at me. He is bidding farewell to his table.

The kitchen of my new apartment on Diamond has three beveled windows, through which I can see the bluish beginnings of the Bay. Down below, boys in tight jeans and cowboy boots walk dogs with frightening leather collars. To the east is a hill bearing rows of houses, the most startling of which is a deep, lovely shade of purple. Sitting at the new table that totters on its broken leg, I have visions of my own heroism, the lengths to which I will go to restore the naked girl's clothes.

In this vision I go out into my city. I take the dress that was given to me, the dress that fell from the sky. I place a foot upon the walkway, the walkway which exists, truly, and which will not collapse beneath me. I stand above the traffic, clutching the white silk that is prone to falling. At last she arrives. She is naked, as when I left her. She holds one hand over each breast as she steps onto the walkway and moves toward me, her sweet thighs slapping together, her belly beaten pink by the wind. She stretches out her hands to receive the dress, revealing the dark of her nipples, the shadows gathering beneath her breasts. In this city that is mine, this city that I dreamed long before I saw it, on this walkway that I built years ago in my mind, I persuade her.

"Come with me," I say. She takes my hand, and I lead her home. Inside, I touch my mouth to the white instep of her foot, press my fingers into the cushion of her calves, and lay my head upon her stomach, hearing the deep pulse of her womb. Many nights gather beneath her eyelids. Her legs are heavy from dreaming. She is a replica of myself from many years ago, before I dreamt of cities and bridges. On the dress that fell away, the dress she sent down to me, I detect my own smell, the print of my own fingers.

I sit at the table and gaze out at my city, dreaming of the rescue. I spread the dress on the table and touch the soft grain of the silk, a blue stain the size of a quarter just above the lower hem. I wrap the dress around me, tie a good knot that will hold, and stand in front of the long window that faces the street. The 37-Corbett clatters by, spewing soot within inches of my window. The passengers cling to straps that hang from the ceiling, lurching forward as the bus comes to a halt; several of them gaze morosely into my kitchen. A man in the back of the bus catches my eye. For a moment I believe it could be Ivan, with his dark bushy hair and half smile, his gentle face. I wave, but he turns away, as if I am not a woman with whom he had intimate relations, as if he didn't beg me, years ago, not to leave him. But a certain unfamiliar movement of the neck, the way this man

THE GIRL IN THE FALL-AWAY DRESS

tilts his chin up toward the ceiling, tells me that the man on the bus is not Ivan.

With my new binoculars I examine the table, each crack a canyon at thirty-two times magnification. Then I point the binoculars out the window at my new city, half hoping to find Ivan among the flower shops and fruit stands lining Eighteenth Street. I scan the horizon and locate the purple house on the hill across Eureka Valley. The front yard has a narrow, sloping flower bed with no flowers, only a thick craggy blanket of ice plants, their sharp fronds glowing a milky green. Back home in Mobile the plush lawns blaze with pink azalea bushes, wisteria drips from the fence-posts, and it is almost too much to take in—all that color and heat. But here the air is cool, the vegetation manageable, and I know that I can make a home here. I resolve to be the first member of my family to leave the South and stay gone.

I think of my mother at another fruit stand in this very city, some thirty years ago, her hands traveling over ripe mounds of tangerines. She sees my father's eager face beneath a sailor's cap; he is running toward her. As he lifts the cap from his head and begins to call her name, she drops three tangerines into a paper sack, presses a quarter into the vendor's open palm, and turns away. In the end, following the advice of her own mother, she will come back to him; but in that moment at the fruit stand my mother is alone and fearless. Walking away, she thinks of all the places she'll go without him. She turns a corner, and my father's voice fades beneath the low howl of a fog horn. In that instant she forgets him. She is not my mother. She is no one's wife. She is a woman set free in her new city, thousands of miles from home.

I think of a story my mother used to tell when we girls would ask how she met our father. In the story she is fourteen years old. Late one night she goes to the kitchen for a glass of water. There she sees a stranger sleeping, his body laid full across the table. She is startled, but then she realizes the stranger is the son of the couple with whom her family shares a house. He has come home for Thanksgiving. He sleeps on his back, arms folded over his stomach. He is wearing a button-down shirt and long pants. He has no sheet or pillow. She moves quietly to the table, peers into his face. His mouth is closed, his breath even. His eyes are still beneath the lids. He does not snore and drool like her brothers, does not jerk in his sleep like her father. He looks as though he came straight out of the pages of *The Elegant Life*. In the magazine, slender ladies in pastel dresses stand on wide verandas, gazing out into the distance. There is always a handsome man standing beside the lady, sipping something cool from a glass, one hand tucked into the pocket of his well-pressed trousers.

My mother lifts the kitchen curtain to see the stranger better in the moonlight. His skin is smooth and tan. He opens his eyes without a yawn, without a stretch. He wakes as elegantly as he sleeps, and seems only slightly surprised to see her standing over him.

"Who are you?" he asks.

"I live here," she says, holding her arms over her chest, suddenly aware of the thinness of her nightshirt.

"Going to a party?" he asks.

"No."

"Then why the fancy do?" He reaches up and tugs at the pink sponge roller around which my mother has rolled her bangs. The sponge comes away in his hand, still wrapped with a strand of her hair.

"I have school pictures tomorrow," she says, embarrassed.

"What grade are you in?"

"Tenth."

"That's a nice grade." He says it in a voice no man or boy has ever used with her. "Will you marry me?"

She does not even pause to consider. "Yes," she says, believing that he was sent to her. The next day at breakfast, he hardly looks her way. Monday morning he is gone. It will be years before they meet again at someone else's wedding, years before he asks her a second time, "Will you marry me?"

Until then, she remains single and somewhat independent, a sleepy tenth grader with puffed-up bangs on page thirty-nine of her year book, an eleventh grader holding a 4H medal in a wrinkled photograph taken at the Lincoln County Fair, a high school senior wearing a piece of cardboard shaped like Italy in her graduation play. Italy is a bit misshapen and Venice a little low in the boot, but my mother knows she has time to get it right. She'll go to Rome and sample the gelato. She'll stand in front of the Leaning Tower of Pisa, and have someone take a photo of her leaning in the wrong direction.

The geography teacher is standing in the wings, motioning frantically for Spain to get in place. My mother nudges her friend Mary, who is wearing an ill-proportioned cardboard cut-out of Spain, and whispers, "You're supposed to be downstage of France." She feels sorry for all those girls whose futures bear the mark of permanence —children and husbands already decided upon. Mary is engaged to be married. Elizabeth was supposed to be the Netherlands, but she's six months gone and showing. My mother can no more imagine her own flat belly growing round than she can imagine a massive silver-gray bridge spanning the frigid waters of San Francisco Bay. The chorus is naming all the countries of Europe to the tune of *America the Beautiful*—Belgium, Romania, Portugal, Albania. For my mother, a confident twelfth grader with a B+ average in geography, the countries sound exotic, but not out of reach. She looks out at the audience, but it's too dark to see any faces. Still, she knows her parents are out there; her mother is wearing heels, her father his Sunday suit. *Italy*, the chorus sings. She steps forward and salutes.